Claudia Chase has a post-graduate Diploma in English Language Teaching, Methodology and Materials Design. She taught countless au pairs towards the Cambridge Exams as well as adult immigrants. In her free time, she enjoyed walking several of Britain's long-distance paths. When she turned 50, she took one year's unpaid leave, packed her rucksack and travelled around the world, with memorable stays in New Zealand and Samoa. This is her first novel. She lives in London.

To my family

Claudia Chase

TWO'S COMPANY...

AUSTIN MACAULEY PUBLISHERS™

LONDON • CAMBRIDGE • NEW YORK • SHARJAH

A CIP catalogue record for this title is available from the British Library.

ISBN 9781398411401 (Paperback)
ISBN 9781398414235 (ePub e-book)

www.austinmacauley.com

First Published 2023
Austin Macauley Publishers Ltd®
1 Canada Square
Canary Wharf
London
E14 5AA

A big thank you to Ian Richardson, Gesine Schmidt and Susan Montague who encouraged me and made helpful suggestions.

Sigh no more, ladies, sigh no more,
Men were deceivers ever,
One foot in sea, and one on shore,
To one thing constant never.
Then sigh not so, but let them go,
And be you blithe and bonny,
Converting all your sounds of woe,
Into hey nonny, nonny.

Sing no more ditties, sing no more,
Of dumps so dull and heavy.
The fraud of men was ever so,
Since summer first was leafy.
Then sigh not so, but let them go,
And be you blithe and bonny,
Converting all your sounds of woe,
Into hey nonny, nonny.

—Much Ado About Nothing, William Shakespeare

TWO'S COMPANY

1

Heather Shilling was standing in her bedroom. She was wearing a beige twinset and the trousers from her tweed trouser suit. She only put her pearl necklace on when she went out. The poppies and cornflowers seemed to be smiling down at her from the wallpaper. She was moving lightly. She opened the door to the wardrobe. It no longer creaked: Jonathan had seen to that.

Out of an anaemic white cardboard box which had been resting at the bottom of the wardrobe like in a vault, she exhumed their wedding photo in its silver frame. She smiled at her younger self who beamed with naivety and trust into a future, *by Jonathan's side* as it would have been described in her favourite kind of novel. The picture showed her looking gorgeous, with her long blond curls. Now, nearly fifteen years later, her hair was mousy and cut short. She envied herself for how she once looked. How could she have let herself go and put on so much weight? She sighed. It was not as if she had not regained her figure after childbirth. She and Jonathan had no children. She quickly deleted these thoughts and marvelled at Jonathan in the photo. Her darling looked so smart in his grey, tight-fitting tail-coat which showed off the athletic body he once had. Clutching the matching top hat, his face wore a proud smile, like that of a ringmaster.

She put the photo where it used to stand, on the bedside table, on her side of the bed. The afternoon sun twinkled on her wedding ring. Heather was glad that she had never taken it off since that day, almost fifteen years ago, which was frozen in the framed photo.

The house in Milton-under-Wychwood was listed as of historical significance and known as *The Old Smithy*. The old anvil was still in an outbuilding in the garden. The sleepy village had a church and a pub as well as a library which was set up in a former shop.

It was a Monday in early March after their return from their second honeymoon in the sun, or so Heather saw it. Escaping from the grey colours and shivery damp cold of England in the middle of February had been such a luxury, but that had been nothing compared to luxuriating in the knowledge of having mended their fraught relationship. After all, they had been divorced for over two years, preceded by a year's separation and bitter fighting. However, Jonathan's shotgun, some of his books and even clothes had been awaiting their removal by him in vain and had been a constant bitter reminder to her of their time together in this house. They had also signalled that Jonathan would return at least once more to collect his belongings.

After three years he had returned, not to collect more of his belongings but for good, from the much younger woman, Carol Costa who he had left her for! Heather had felt rewarded for her tenacity and perseverance in her belief that a marriage was forever, with or without a divorce, even if she had been the one to instigate it! She knew this defied the laws of logic almost as much as continuing to wear her wedding ring despite her divorce.

At least there she had been able to think of one good reason to leave it on her finger. She started running a Bed and Breakfast establishment after the divorce in the former matrimonial home in this picturesque Cotswold village, and sometimes she had gentlemen travelling on their own staying with her. She wanted the ring to ward them off, and it had worked!

She needed to earn money to pay off the enormous loan she had to take out after the divorce in order to pay Jonathan half his share in the property. Heather had rejected the alternative of selling up, splitting the proceeds and moving into a much smaller house somewhere. Her intuition had told her, and Jonathan's appearance confirmed that she had been right, that a return to her would be coupled with the lure of the very place Jonathan had invested so much time and work in, had to be linked with this physical symbol of a country gentleman's lifestyle, the large garden, the fields and the small wood, not least the barn and stables he built himself. Also, she had not been able to face up to life without Jonathan and part with her horse as well. Nowhere she could have moved with half of the proceeds from the sale of their house, would she have had the facilities of stabling her horse, Dinah.

Jonathan had thought of a clause in the divorce settlement whereby she had to agree to forego any claim on his pension for a one-off payment of £ 50,000, which was also to be in lieu of maintenance. Heather had been outraged at this because Jonathan had also wanted her to sign the following: should she start living with another partner, married or not married to him, during the first five years after the divorce, she would have to repay him £ 10,000 per year for cohabiting with someone else.

Jonathan had always been crafty, used to driving hard bargains. After months of wrangling and quarrelling with him via their respective solicitors, her forceful and determined female solicitor had succeeded in making sure that no conditions were attached to the one-off payment of £ 50,000.

She thought of all the bitterness that had been between them over the years and switched to thinking on how they could now rewrite the script for their resumed life together. She had been determined to be the main author of this script, ever since Jonathan suddenly burst back into her life when he knocked on the door of, *The Old Smithy,* in Milton-under-Wychwood. She had felt triumphant at seeing him stand there unannounced on that freezing evening of New Year's Day, smiling shyly and looking bedraggled.

'Are you going to ask me in?'

Just hearing Jonathan's voice had dented her conviction that she had managed to feel at ease with life on her own in the years since their split. How she had missed him since he moved out to live with Carol and her two daughters, though at odd moments she had caught herself not having thought about him. This had always startled her with an unwanted feeling of guilt, mixed with a wished-for sensation of an independence she had not known for years, not since before she had met him.

'Happy New Year, Heather,' Jonathan had whispered her name and paused to let the effect take hold of her, 'I badly need to talk to you, please, let me in.'

He had smiled at her awkwardly, tilting his head a little. Heather had moved back from the door to let Jonathan walk ahead into the living room, raising his head to look at the familiar pictures of hunting scenes in the hallway. Without being invited to do so, he had sat down on the sofa in front of the enormous fireplace. Heather had followed him and sunk into an armchair nearby. Staring at him like an apparition, she had felt utter confusion: hadn't she been secretly waiting for this moment all this time while encouraging these feelings of independence to grow in her?

I mustn't make it easy for him, she thought to herself.

'Who do you think you are, just turning up like that! You're compromising me. You could at least have phoned me first.'

Heather's voice had sounded harsh and irritated, but her body was speaking another language. Especially her eyes were begging him to say something to erase all the hurt he had dealt out to her in the past.

'I know this is most unexpected, Heather, and it has taken me all my courage to come and ask you this. This is not easy to say, but Heather, will you have me back? It is a lot to hope for, almost too much, I know, to count on your forgiveness…'

'Wait a minute, it has taken me all this time to get you out of my system.'

Heather had interrupted him. She needed to put up a barricade. She expected it of herself.

'And you come barging into my life just like that and think you can pick up where you left off…'

'Heather, listen, it isn't quite as you say. For the last few months, I've been thinking about you, and I know now I made the biggest mistake of my life when I left you.'

14

He checked for a relaxation of her facial muscles like a skilful anaesthetist. Heather needed another dose, and she actually told him which one.

'What went wrong between you and Carol? Don't tell me you left just out of remorse.' Jonathan had to get his response right.

'Carol just hasn't got your maturity, Heather, she even used to get jealous if I was just five minutes late. We had one of our many arguments over that if you want to know another reason why I left her.'

Jonathan had moved, bit by bit, closer to the armchair Heather had retreated into and blocked the exit by crouching on the floor, with his hand on Heather's knee. He had been as overcome by emotion as Heather had by the power given to her. And if you're in a powerful position, wasn't it the noblest thing to be merciful?

'Heather, please, please, if you can find it in your heart, forgive me for the pain I've caused you.'

As she leant forward and reached for his hands, Jonathan added pleadingly, 'I'll do anything you'll ask me, Heather, to have you back. I need you. I need you because I love you. I've never really stopped loving you…'

Jonathan knew it well, these words were the passport across the final frontier into Heather's heart, and, rightly calculated, Heather had been only too aware of her need to believe him. Only that would make sense of her life and for the many years Jonathan had played the key role in it already. They were going to put their relationship right once and for all.

'Jonathan, I've never stopped loving you either. You will have to promise me to make one last, all-out effort to make our relationship work. You know what that means, don't you? I want you to promise absolute and lasting faithfulness to me and to wear your wedding ring again from now on.'

Jonathan had no clue as to where he had put his wedding ring when he had taken it off while he was living with Carol. He'd have to start a search. It might be with his gold cufflinks. He very much hoped so. If not, he'd have to hunt for exactly the same ring again in jewellers' shops, and what would be more, he'd have to have the inside of the ring inscribed with Heather's name and the date of their wedding, just as Heather's ring was inscribed with Jonathan's name and their wedding date.

He shuddered but said, 'I promise, Heather, I have no hesitation!'

Jonathan had been overjoyed with Heather's willingness to give him this chance, against all the odds. They had hugged and kissed and cried.

'How about the two of us celebrating our reconciliation, Heather, what would you say about a couple of weeks in the sun together somewhere? I've got some accrued holidays from mid-February! You don't have many guests at that time of year, do you, anyway? How many are staying here right now?'

'None at all, which isn't unusual for the Christmas and New Year's period.'

'Leave the booking to me.'

They had ended up in the Dominican Republic, and Jonathan's 40th birthday fell into this holiday, perfect timing for sharing this special day, which Jonathan could not have faced on his own. Jonathan had booked the trip at a travel agency in Abingdon, and as usual, managed to wrangle all sorts of concessions and reductions in price out of the owner. It was just as well that she was not a mere employee there. His usual charm attack had worked again. He was much relieved when the wedding ring had turned up, not with his cufflinks but in his toolbox. It was a chance discovery, and he had no idea how it had got there. He had felt very self-conscious wearing it during their trip.

Natalie, the teenage daughter of Heather's neighbours, a trustworthy, skilful and keen young horse woman, was overjoyed at having a daily chance of riding out on Dinah, Heather's horse, in return for mucking out the stable, feeding, watering and brushing her while Heather and Jonathan were away.

The holiday had gone well, Heather thought. They had walked around hand in hand, had refined their lovemaking from the awkward way it had resumed after his arrival that January night. They had found plenty to talk about, pointing out things to each other in this new place. It had done them good to be far away from the pressures of everyday life. He had been attentive to her, had showered her with compliments on her looks and her good taste in clothes.

Two days after their return from their holiday, Jonathan had to be in London for a two-week work assignment, to cover several important sports matches for the radio station where he had worked as a sound engineer since the age of eighteen. Before he left for London, he asked Heather if she wanted to give up the bed and breakfast business now. It sounded as if he wanted her to give it up. He was not keen on meeting strangers on the stairs, in the hallway, least of all at the breakfast or dinner table as Heather had gathered from some murmured comments he had made. She was again thinking of her determination to write the script of their new life together and decided to stand her ground.

'Jonathan, you're away so often, and I've become used to having people around and enjoy my chats with guests. It cheers me up. Also, the B&B has really picked up, and it would be a pity to close it down after all the effort I put into it. What I suggest is that you give me your work schedule a month in advance, and we can compromise. I won't accept any bookings for the times when you're at home.'

Jonathan thought this quite sensible, so Heather scored a win. Jonathan then wanted to talk about the loan Heather had taken out and had been repaying monthly to the bank for the last two years.

'I've been thinking that you should perhaps continue to pay the loan back for the next, say, few months, Heather, while we both make sure we're happy with our resumed relationship. And if so, I will be pleased to pay the remaining loan back to your bank as a lump sum from the share of the house I've already received. It goes without saying that the deeds of the house will then again have to be in both our names. What do you say?'

Heather principally agreed but said she wanted to mull it over. She would ask him if she had any further questions.

Heather was used to these absences, which had been an integral part of their marriage.

What a difference it makes to be on your own when you know you're part of a couple, Heather thought and revelled in this feeling of not having to wait in vain for Jonathan's return.

'The wedding photo looks just right in its old place again. This will please Jonathan when he next comes home,' Heather told herself with satisfaction. 'It's really working this time, we're together again for good, after all.'

2

In the late spring of about three years ago, Jonathan and Heather had been invited to a party in a nearby village, given by friends of theirs, Stella and Steven. When they arrived, they found the front door open and so marched straight in. It was a lively gathering of professional people on that warm late spring night who had mostly arrived in couples though there were a few singles drifting about. As soon as Jonathan entered the living room by Heather's side, his eyes were roaming to spot any attractive woman, and yes, looking over Heather's shoulder, there was one who stood out from the crowd. She was tall and slim though curvy, in a revealing purple dress with a black blazer, with glossy auburn hair which cascaded down her back, and with a brilliant smile. His purple woman, if not scarlet, was quite a bit younger than Heather. He could hardly drag his eyes away.

He wanted to check out the garden and its terrace with the same objective in mind, but Heather clung to him like a limpet.

'Oh, darling, would you mind very much getting a glass of gin and tonic for each of us?' Jonathan asked Heather. 'I just want to find our hosts Steven and Stella to let them know we've arrived.' And she complied and walked towards the crowded drinks table.

Jonathan swiftly took his wedding ring off by sheer habit and slipped it into his pocket. He entered the garden and not long after, that gorgeous woman he had spotted before stepped out as well, accompanied by two men. Jonathan strolled over to their group, said 'hello' and asked how they knew the hosts.

'Oh, Carol here is a friend of our host's, she went to school with Stella,' one of the men said, 'and Jasper and I belong to Steven's cricket team in the village.'

Just then Steven appeared, looking flustered. 'Jasper, can you help me open that keg of beer you brought along, please? It's in the garage.' And with that, the three men left Carol standing there with Jonathan.

He, forever the joker, asked her, 'Do you come here often?'

She scowled at that. 'Is that your usual chat-up line?'

She took her blazer off and flung it on an empty chair. Jonathan could hardly avert his eyes from Carol's cleavage and was beginning to feel dizzy. He asked her if she'd come far, and it turned out she only lived a short drive away. She was holding a drink in her hand from which she took small sips from time to time. He noticed that her glass was nearly empty.

'Is your husband getting you another drink?' he asked.

Carol flinched but told Jonathan that she was separated from her husband. That was the confirmation Jonathan had been hoping for. Only then did Jonathan look at her left ring finger where he could not detect a wedding ring.

I hope Heather will still be quite a while with those drinks and give me more time with this temptress, he thought and continued to ogle Carol.

Jonathan, an expert at flirtation, asked her, 'Have you got a licence for that dress?'

Carol laughed out aloud, then countered, 'What on earth do you mean? Are you wearing that Hawaiian shirt for a bet?'

Jonathan went on with the banter, 'Well, there seems to be an atomic fallout of your weapons of mass distraction.'

'Don't think for a moment I'd hula with you.'

'Who says I'd want to?'

'Your eyes give the game away.'

'Oh, I see you've been looking deeply into my eyes, the windows of my soul.'

'I can't see any soul, but I can hear soul music indoors.'

They continued in this way, and Carol flirted outrageously with words and with gestures, until Jonathan spotted Heather at the door into the garden quite a while later, clutching two glasses.

'Excuse me a moment,' he said. 'Don't go away, whatever you do!'

'Oh,' Carol said, 'I didn't seem to catch your name.'

'It's Jonathan, by the way,' he said and hastened to slip his wedding ring on again unseen and turned towards Heather and indoors to avoid having to introduce the two women to each other.

After standing around with Heather indoors for a while, they spotted some acquaintances and chatted with them.

'Oh, hello, Fred, how are you doing, old mate? Yes, I know, long time, no see…well, you know how much my job takes me away…'

'Lovely to see you, Heather! How are you? It's been a while, hasn't it? We must meet up sometime soon to catch up properly. Have you still got your horse? I imagine it keeps you busy, or have you started a job since we last saw each other?'

'Yes, Jane, I still ride out every day, come rain or shine, but I can't really face a job which takes me away from the house most of the day, and there's enough to do with the garden as well.'

What seemed like a long time later, Jonathan said to Heather, 'I'll just see if the beer keg has been opened.' And slipped briefly into the garage, and there he quickly scribbled a note to Carol in the momentarily deserted garage: *'I must see you again, gorgeous Carol, please give me a ring on mobile 03754 942 156. J.'*

Heather stayed by his side most of the evening. Her antennae seemed to be quivering.

How can I get rid of her for a few moments? Jonathan thought, *I want to check if Carol is still in the garden, or if other men are chatting her up.*

Finally, Stella had beckoned Heather over to her. 'At long last, Stella! Let me tell you what a pleasant party this is, and such a perfect summer evening. Jonathan and I've just been chatting to Fred and Jane, and it's lovely to see them again.'

Jonathan immediately dashed into the darkened garden. It took some moments for his eyes to adjust to the sparsely lit terrace and seek out Carol who was sitting chatting with another woman. Jonathan approached the chair she was sitting on from behind and slipped his note into the pocket of Carol's blazer, unnoticed by her.

Fingers crossed that she'll find it soon, and even more that she will phone me!

On the drive back home, Jonathan asked Heather who was at the wheel if she had enjoyed the party. Her answer was not overenthusiastic. Large parties just were not her scene. At home, Heather soon changed into one of her usual cotton nighties the colour of innocence, and Jonathan was relieved to blame too much alcohol for his lack of amorous advances. His thoughts and fantasies were focussed on Carol, the temptress in purple.

Days went by without any phone call from Carol, and Jonathan was bothered by the silence of the phone not ringing. He was about to give up hope after a week had passed. He couldn't really ask Stella and Steven for Carol's phone number without arousing suspicion. So, the game would be lost... Then, one evening ten days after the party, when he was working away from home for several days, his mobile phone rang, and to his delight, he heard Carol's voice.

'It's Carol here, you scoundrel, I've only just found the note you smuggled into the pocket of my blazer. After the party, I only wore that blazer again a few days ago. What does all this mean?'

Jonathan told her that she'd deprived him of sleep, and how she could make that up to him by meeting him again and asked her where she lived.

She said in Wallingford, and Jonathan instantly thought, *That's half-way between the Cotswolds and London. Perfect, not too close to Milton-under-Wychwood, and also on my commute from there to where most of my work takes me, London.*

'Would you do me the honour of letting me invite you for dinner in Wallingford next week?'

'My God, that almost sounds like a marriage proposal!' Carol exclaimed. 'But to get back to practicalities, I'll have to get my neighbour to look in on my children. What day are you thinking of?'

'How many children do you have?'

'Two, two girls.'

'Ah, how lovely. How old are they?'

'Eleven and thirteen.'

'Wonderful, you're so lucky! How about next Wednesday evening? Give me your address, and I'll pick you up at 7:30.'

3

On Wednesday, time seemed to crawl for Jonathan. He and his team were working in Oxford that week, which was very convenient, with Wallingford not far away. He had researched online for the poshest restaurant in this small town. Actually, it was a historic 17th-century pub called, *the Barley Mow*, famous for its food and atmosphere. He had reserved a table in a cosy corner.

When he turned up at Carol's address, her two daughters were peering out through the window until told off by their mother. Immediately upon entering Carol's house, Jonathan felt wrapped up in a warm family atmosphere because the kitchen and living room came across as truly lived-in, though not messy spaces. The interior was cleverly designed, with stylish furniture and subtle colours and evocative pictures on the walls. The sofa was grass green, and the cushions were violet which looked simply stunning. Especially Lisa, the older daughter, could not stop giggling at his jokes, and Cara, the younger one, wanted to show Jonathan the paintings she had done at school. Jonathan felt included, he actually felt victorious at not being treated like an intruder at all. Carol looked mesmerising, her hair was shiny, her make-up immaculate, and her smile was warm and inviting.

'You can stay up another hour, girls,' said Carol, 'but then you'll have to go to bed. Mrs Walker next door is going to look in on you in a while. Give me a kiss and sleep well! You've got school tomorrow morning!'

Jonathan played the perfect gentleman in the pub, pulling the chair out for Carol to sit on.

'Carol, you look simply gorgeous, and my heartbeat is going up. Phew! Do tell me a bit more about yourself. Have you been living here in Wallingford for long?'

'Yes, quite a while, ever since my husband and I separated two years ago.'

'Do you go out to work, Carol? Or are you a lady who lunches?'

'I'm the school secretary at my girls' school. It's a fab job because I'm on holiday when they are, and I also really like my job. But tell me about yourself. What do you do?'

'I'm a sound engineer for radio, and my team records most of the international and other sports matches, so I'm often away from home for a week or longer at times.'

'Where is home?' Carol asked.

'I have a lovely house in Milton-under-Wychwood in the Cotswolds.'

'At the party I got the impression that you were there as a single, Jonathan, well, let's say I didn't notice a wedding ring on your finger or see you arrive or leave with any female. And I haven't spoken to Stella or Steve since the party, so haven't had a chance to ask about you...'

'You know, lots of married men don't wear a wedding ring and its absence should not lead to conclusions. I'm spoken for actually, but I must confess to you that I'm not all that happy in my marriage.'

A warning light came on in Carol's head.

Oh no, not another man who will tell me that his wife doesn't understand him, she thought.

'We've been together for such a long time, and it just happens sometimes that you end up in a rut, everything is predictable and therefore quite boring. I also wish my wife didn't just stay in the house as a homemaker. It would be better for her and me if she had a job outside the house. She has lost a lot of self-confidence over the years and feels safest at home.'

'Are there any children?' Carol asked.

Jonathan sighed, pulled a sad face and said, 'Alas, no, and that has caused a lot of grief in our marriage.'

The two of them probed into their past and present lives and tossed censored morsels of information to each other, not unlike a game of tennis. Their hands happened to meet on the table time and again. The food was delicious, and they drank copious glasses of expensive French wine. It certainly helped them to see each other in the best of lights. It was just as well that they had come on foot from Carol's house. But Jonathan had to drive back to Oxford, which was quite risky after so many glasses of wine, so much so that Carol became concerned.

'Jonathan, I'd be doing something illegal if I let you drive that sort of distance after all that wine. Listen, you can sleep on the living room sofa as long as you leave early in the morning so that my daughters won't see you.'

'As long as you give me a good night kiss too, Carol,' Jonathan begged, and for quite a while, they became entangled with each other on the sofa.

When he left at six in the morning, he knew he had irredeemably fallen in love with Carol and had to see her again. And again…

4

Several days after the party, Heather saddled her horse, Dinah, and was looking forward to riding along the fields and then through the nearby woods. She always found that this was the perfect time to do her thinking. It was so lovely to breathe pure country air without pollution from cars and to be surrounded by nature, to listen to the birds singing and the leaves rustling in the faint breeze.

Let me count my blessings, she thought, *I have a really smart husband I love but don't see as often as I'd like because of his job, but still, we have this beautiful home in the country, a real country person's residence with four bedrooms, a large garden with fruit trees and flowers, I have my own horse and can indulge in my favourite pastime, riding, whenever I want. If only he stopped nagging me to find a job outside the house! How long have we been married now? Let me see, for nearly twelve years, unbelievable!*

Suddenly, Heather had to think of her greatest sorrow as well, so had to stop counting any more blessings.

The greatest pain still is that our marriage has remained childless, oh, how it still hurts! Neither of us even thought of having a medical check-up before we tied the knot, and none of our friends did either, it simply didn't cross our minds. I was twenty-seven and Jonathan was twenty-five when we got married and moved into a small flat in London, and we wanted to save for a deposit for our house, so we decided that I would continue to work as a museum guard to help scrape the money together. So, we postponed having children for another two years. And then, we hoped, before I hit the age of thirty, we'd be parents, oh, of a little boy or girl! After those two years, we bought our house here together, leaving London behind, to live in a safer and healthier part of the country for families. Well, it just didn't happen. I never became pregnant. I wasn't too thrown at first because it was a busy time to get the nursery painted, choose the little cot, sew the bed linen for it, beautifully printed fabrics in yellow, fine for either a baby boy or baby girl, get the entire house redecorated, the curtains sewn, the garden designed and planted, to meet the new neighbours and settle in a different community. But after the first two years in the new house, I started to wonder if anything was wrong, and I mentioned my worries to Jonathan, didn't I? And he immediately suggested that I should get myself checked out! Me! I remember too well how I felt his accusing finger pointing at me! It takes two to tango! He just wouldn't accept at first that something might not be in order with him, his Lordship! I was immediately ready to consult an obstetrician. It might take a lot of arguing and quarrelling to finally make an appointment with a doctor for Jonathan, though. And lo and behold, there was and is nothing wrong with me.

5

Heather urged Jonathan:

'Jonathan, my darling, we can't just ignore this situation. We'll have to get to the bottom of it for both our sakes. Please, pick up the phone and make an appointment with Doctor Mountfield. Perhaps you can be seen before you've got to work away again.'

With a heavy heart, and under pressure from Heather, Jonathan made an appointment with their GP who referred him to a specialist at the local hospital. When he and Heather both came in for the results of tests, the specialist asked Jonathan, 'Tell me, have you ever had mumps as a child?'

'Yes, I remember how glad I was at the time to miss some days at school,' Jonathan said nonchalantly, 'I must have been eight or nine years old. Why do you ask?'

'Well, this can be a serious matter,' Professor Dutton continued. 'In some cases, it can leave a man infertile, and in fact, your semen sample confirms that your sperm count is extremely low. You told me that you two have been trying in vain for a baby for the last two years, and that, indeed, is another indicator that your infertility is at the bottom of it.'

Jonathan's eyes became shiny, and Heather's filled with tears.

This was a sentence worse than any court of law could pronounce. They held each other by their hands, more upset than ever before.

Does this professor not have any nicer bedside manner? Does he have to be so blunt? Jonathan thought.

'Is there any course of action you could advise?' he asked in a shaky voice, feeling absolutely shattered.

'You and your wife could consider artificial insemination, of course,' the professor answered.

'Oh, how do you mean? You've just told me that my sperm count is very low and that I'm likely to be infertile!' Jonathan shouted.

'Please, calm down, Mr Shilling, and let me explain. Many couples have resorted to the method of artificial insemination for the wife to get pregnant, the sperm would be from a donor.'

Jonathan jumped up at hearing this, his face red, his eyes wide open with shock.

'I would recommend that you and your wife go home and discuss this possibility in peace and quiet. It really is not the end of the world, you know. Of course, you could also consider adoption...'

'Never, never,' Jonathan cried, 'neither of these children would have my DNA!'

Heather tried to calm him down, thanked the specialist and pulled Jonathan to the door by the hand. In the car, they had to wait for a while before Jonathan was calm enough to drive them home.

6

Jonathan initially avoided any discussions on what the professor had suggested as options. Whenever Heather mentioned that they should talk about them, he asked her to stop speaking or simply left the room. Heather could see how shaken and even offended Jonathan was by this new self-image of a man who could not father any offspring. Several days later, as they were sitting in front of the fireplace, Jonathan turned the TV off and said that he was now ready for a talk.

'Let's get it over and done with,' he said in a tired tone.

He asked Heather for her thoughts.

'I never ever contemplated going through life without having children. That thought is impossible for me, having children is my calling in life, and therefore I would certainly contemplate opting for artificial insemination or adoption. Look, Jonathan, this is incredibly important to me, and even if the child only has the DNA from one of us or even neither of us in the case of adoption, both of us would love that child and be happy as a family and fulfil a dream!'

'I can't tell you how shattered I am at this news, Heather, especially as we are now finally ready to have a family, with a house in an idyllic setting in the country. But I really draw the line at these proposals by the professor and won't have you artificially inseminated with another guy's sperm. Good heavens, you don't know what sort of character the donor is as a person and therefore what we're letting ourselves in for. And mark my words, adoption is even more out of the question for me! What if the child wants to search for its birth parents in teenage or whenever!'

'Listen, Jonathan, adoption would be the best option from my point of view because it would be fair on two counts, first of all, giving a child a family and home, and secondly, perhaps even more importantly, this child would neither have my nor your DNA, in all fairness! I've waited so long and am now nearly thirty-one, I now need a child to look after for my own sanity, especially as you're away so often for days on end for work! Please, please, Jonathan!'

'Heather, once and for all, no, no, no! I now regard this topic as closed for good. Don't ever mention it to me again. If you want a child that much, you will have to leave this marriage and find yourself a fertile man. Make up your mind, and before I go to work tomorrow, let me know your decision!'

'How can you be so cruel, you can't mean that, Jonathan! I love you the most in the world and will never want to be without you. There, that's my answer to your absurd choice! But remember that I will never get over not having a child.'

That night, as they climbed into the barren field of a marriage bed, they turned their backs to each other and barely wished each other a good night.

The next day, Jonathan had to work in London for six days. It was the end of October, and this autumn was splendid, with fog in the early mornings and sunshine later in the day.

The woods were touched by warm colours, with the leaves turning golden, red and brown. Heather had done a lot of gardening recently, collected broken branches, old planks and dry leaves and piled them up for a bonfire at the bottom of the garden for bonfire night. The pile was getting bigger, it would be a splendid sight, once it was alight. Heather expected Jonathan home in the afternoon of November 5th, when it would be dark already.

She waited and waited, it was already after six o'clock, and he still had not come home, nor had he phoned her. So, she decided to go ahead and light the bonfire. It was beginning to burn down faster than she had thought.

What else can I put on the fire? she wondered, and on an impulse dashed into the house, went upstairs and dragged the baby cot down the stairs, out of the back door to the bottom of the garden.

She found the axe and wielded it with a strength she did not know she had, panting and screaming and screeching, howling with each blow as the wood split, sobbing and crying. And this way she burnt her life's dream. She stood exhausted and watched the fire first flare up, then burn down while it started to rain heavily. She scarcely noticed how she got soaked, with her wet hair clinging to her head and her mascara running down her cheeks. Finally, feeling weak and dizzy, registering at last what she had done, she limped through the dark garden to the back door into the kitchen.

Jonathan looked up as she stumbled in and collapsed on the floor. The fridge door was open, and he was helping himself to some cheese and was about to pull a bottle of white wine from the top shelf. He almost dropped the bottle as he went to crouch down beside Heather.

'Heather, what's the matter, what happened? You're all wet, and you smell of smoke, where have you been?'

Heather needed several minutes to stop sobbing before being able to speak.

'I burnt the baby's cot on the bonfire! There won't ever be a baby! I burnt the baby's cot, do you understand, Jonathan? We will stay childless for the rest of our lives. That's what you wanted, isn't it!'

Jonathan tried to hug her, but she pushed him away and only allowed him to help her get up. She went upstairs, had a shower, and by the time he entered their bedroom she was either asleep or pretending to be. Jonathan had never seen Heather beside herself like that and finally comprehended how wounded she was at the realisation that they would never have any children.

When he woke up the next morning, her side of the bed was empty. He searched for her in the house and garden, and when he saw that Dinah was not in her stable, he finally realised that Heather was out riding.

Time passed, initially Heather tended to wear black clothes, and Jonathan thought flippantly *as if in mourning*. But Heather was indeed deeply mourning someone who did not exist and never would, she was mourning her empty womb. She suffered from depression, never smiled, and felt totally left alone during Jonathan's many absences. She started taking anti-depressants on the advice of her doctor, cried a lot, and neglected her housework as well as herself. When Jonathan was at home, he was intent on spending a lot of time in the garden or shed in order not to be in the same room too much with Heather. They ran out of things to say to each other. Jonathan disliked having to go home and ended up volunteering to fill slots for colleagues who had reported sick. They were almost leading separate lives.

Finally, Jonathan saw the danger signs.

'Heather, let's make an effort to enjoy some things together when I'm home,' he suggested, 'let's go out to eat sometimes so you don't have to cook. Also, there's a horse show on at Newmarket, surely, you'd love to see that!'

Her recovery from her depression was slow but she was never quite the same again.

Despite the tests and the evidence, Jonathan never wholly believed that he could possibly be infertile and secretly still thought that Heather was at fault.

7

After that first dinner with Carol, Jonathan invented excuse after excuse with Heather.

'Hello?'

'Hello, Heather, it's Jonathan here. I won't be able to come home for my break, I'm afraid. I've been asked to stand in for my colleague Bill who's off sick. I'll keep you posted, and hope Bill will recover soon. Will you be okay?'

'Oh, no, Jonathan, not again! I wish someone else could take over from Bill. I'm so longing to have you here!'

'It just can't be helped, Heather. We'll have to grin and bear it. I do hope to see you soon. Bye, my love.'

When Jonathan was not pretending to work to replace a sick colleague, he complained to Heather that he had to work for more days than he really had to, just to spend more time with Carol and her daughters. They had soon accepted him as a substitute father figure, especially as their own father seemed to have forgotten about them. A considerable part of Carol's attraction for Jonathan lay in the fact that she had proved fertile, with two daughters to show for it, apart from thinking her beautiful and fascinating. Also, Carol no longer cared that Jonathan was a married man. He could make her laugh with his witty repartee. Once, standing with her in front of a junk shop in a small town, he said he would have called the shop, *Junk and Disorderly*. Another time, when they ordered Indian food in, he thought the business should have been called, *Abra Kebabra*.

Anyway, she loved his stay with her, she thought that she was in love with him. He was always cheerful. Importantly, Lisa and Cara seemed to like him very much and did not appear to mind that he was sharing their mother's bedroom during his frequent short stays with them. Their relationship had taken off, and it felt to Carol as though she was actually married to him. He had told Carol that he was infertile and that there was no need to take precautions but secretly he was hoping to make Carol pregnant. What a triumph that would be! Well, for him, but perhaps not for her. He would deal with that if it came about in the future.

He moaned about having to make appearances at his own home.

'Oh, Carol, I just loathe leaving you and the girls to go home to Heather who's so boring. I can't help comparing her to you. Do you really think I need to go? I could find another excuse and ring her.'

This went on until Carol could not put up with it any longer.

'Jonathan, I don't understand how you can play this double game. It's high time you pulled yourself together and were open with Heather who isn't suspecting that you've been cheating on her. This is really quite despicable, you know, and is definitely an aspect I don't like about you at all. You need to make up your mind. It's either Heather or me!'

'Oh, Carol, I could never now give you up! Okay, I promise to have that difficult talk with Heather, and of course, absolutely dread her reaction to my suggestion of a formal separation.'

But how could he be honest with Heather? Every time he went home to Heather, he swore he would broach that subject but never managed when he saw how delighted Heather was with his presence.

During one of Jonathan's lengthy absences, Heather arranged to meet up with her friend Stella on a Saturday. A long time, nearly a year, in fact, had passed since the party, during which Stella and Heather had just talked to each other on the phone from time to time. Heather was looking forward to visiting Stella for the afternoon and catching up with her news. Stella and Steven had been to Australia for a couple of months, and she was keen to find out about their adventure travelling the country. Heather had baked some muffins to take along to go with their cups of tea. Steven was playing cricket in an away game in another village. The road led through a beautiful part of the countryside, with fields on one side and ancient trees on the other, and Heather enjoyed the drive. The trees looked like huge sculptures against the sky as if made by artists, their intertwining branches like lace.

Stella had laid the tea table with her mother's pretty old porcelain and had also baked a cake. The two friends sat down, Stella poured the tea, and Heather asked Stella about her latest holidays in Australia. They had absolutely loved their trip around the country.

'How was your trip to Australia, Stella?'

'It was so exciting because it was such a learning curve. We actually saw kangaroos in the wild. Can you imagine? We went wine tasting quite a few times in Western Australia and we even climbed a fire outlook tree which was 200 feet high.

We swam in the ocean and also took some surf boarding lessons.'

'How wonderful! It must have been a trip of a lifetime!' Heather exclaimed but shuddered at the thought of the long flight.

Stella asked Heather how Jonathan was, and Heather immediately sighed and told Stella how little she saw of him these days, less than ever before because he was working so hard.

They also chatted about friends they had in common.

'Have you been in touch with Fred and Jane, Stella? We spoke to them briefly at your party. And we meant to meet up with them again, but we haven't got around to it. Jonathan is hardly at home.'

All of a sudden, Stella blushed and got embarrassed and started stuttering.

'What's the matter, Stella?' asked Heather.

'Oh, Heather, the main reason I've asked you here this afternoon is actually Jonathan. Our friend Jasper, he is in the same cricket team as Steve and lives in this village. I wonder if you met him at our party? I'm telling you this as your friend because I think you should know... Well, Jasper saw Jonathan hand in hand with Carol the other day, somewhere near Wallingford, they seemed very cosy with each other. I'm so, so sorry to give you such news...'

Heather sat without the slightest movement. Her face lost all colour, and she was feeling sick in the pit of her stomach. It barely looked to Stella as if Heather was breathing.

Then finally Heather said with a sob, 'I'm sure Jasper was mistaken. Because if not, this is the end of my world. And who is Carol, anyway? Do you know her, Stella?'

'Yes, she's a friend of ours and was also at our party last year, where she and Jonathan must have met for the first time.'

'I remember your party very distinctly, and especially that Jonathan and I stayed together all the time and didn't mingle separately.'

'Oh, Heather, there must have been a time when he was on his own, however briefly, perhaps when you went to the bathroom or helped yourself from the buffet and started talking to people there. You know how it is.'

'Where does Carol live, Stella, and how old is she?'

Stella, feeling awkward, tried to answer Heather's string of questions as factually as possible.

Heather was feeling dizzy. She dashed to the bathroom, feeling sick, her heart was pounding. She was shaking. She poured water on her hands and dabbed her face. It took her some time to collect herself and return to Stella who looked at her with concern.

'Oh, Heather, sit down here beside me. Perhaps I shouldn't have said anything? Would you rather have stayed ignorant of what's been happening? If so, then I will deeply regret having thrown you into such inner turmoil and apologise for it.'

'It's okay, Stella, you acted as a true friend but it's such a blow if it's true.'

Heather accepted a small brandy before she drove home. So, Carol was five years younger than her, and she, Heather, apparently belonged on the scrap heap! Her mind was poisoned, now full of suspicion, rage, fear and total disappointment, a cauldron of emotions. Was she really supposed to be grateful to Stella for telling her this news?

Well, perhaps, because knowing would give her a clear choice of action, to accept Jonathan's betrayal, or to separate from him. If this was true, why had Jonathan not said anything to her? He'd had nearly a year to do so! She could still pretend not to know what Stella had just told her. Given a choice, would she rather not know and continue to live with her illusion that everything was fine between her and Jonathan? That would amount to living a lie. But if it was true, had he not told her because he was a coward?

'I'll have to confront him next time when he comes home,' she determined.

8

Stella felt awful at seeing Heather so disturbed and upset and decided to give her old school friend Carol a ring to arrange to see her and get to the bottom of the story the very next day. Perhaps Jasper had not recognised Jonathan. After all, the party had been held a year ago, perhaps his eyesight had got worse?

'Carol, it's Stella here. How are you? It's been ages since our last get-together. Listen, will you be free after school on Monday? There's just something I'd like to talk to you about.' 'Yes, I can be with you at 4 pm. See you then, Carol!'

On the drive to Wallingford the following afternoon, Stella was wishing that Jasper had been mistaken, though a lot of hurt had been caused to Heather already. Stella reproached herself for not checking the facts with Carol before having invited Heather over. How could she have been so stupid and negligent?

Carol was beaming when Stella got out of her car in front of Carol's house.

'You look great, Carol!' Stella exclaimed. 'Where are the girls?'

'They are having afternoon tea with schoolmates today.'

Good, perfect, Stella thought, *we can talk without any interruptions.*

Carol led the way into the dining room, made coffee and put out some biscuits.

'How's your job, Carol? Do you still like it?'

'Oh, yes, I really love it. Both the children and the teachers at the school are so very nice.'

'That's good to hear. Listen, Carol, I heard something through the grapevine. You've been spotted in a village near here with Jonathan Shilling, actually holding hands with him. Our friend Jasper mentioned it to Steven, and he, of course, told me. Is there any truth in it?'

'What's this, Stella, the inquisition? I'm not doing anything illegal when I harmlessly hold hands with someone!'

'No, but I'm sure you're doing a bit more than holding hands like a teenager! This "someone" is a married man, Carol. Do you know that?'

'Yes, I do, Jonathan himself told me quite openly.'

'And that doesn't make any difference to you? Jonathan and his wife Heather are friends of ours, and I certainly don't approve.'

'Oh, Stella, you're so old-fashioned. I don't care if he's married or not, and I don't know if he's told his wife or not. We've been an item since shortly after your party, he practically lives here with me and the girls who like him. It's too late to do anything about it because we've fallen in love with each other.'

'Heather now knows, Carol, and not from Jonathan; she's incredibly upset.'

Stella told Carol about Heather's visit and her distress a couple of days earlier.

9

'Hello, darling, how are you?' were Jonathan's first words on entering the house when he next came to stay with Heather.

'I couldn't feel worse,' Heather answered bitterly.

'Oh, why is that? Are you ill?'

'I think there is something you need to tell me, you coward!' Heather shouted. 'Tell me, how is Carol?'

'Hm, what do you mean, which Carol?'

'Oh, come on, own up, Jonathan, don't play games of innocence with me. I heard it through the grapevine. You and Carol have been spotted together. How long has it been going on?'

Jonathan confessed, 'Oh, Heather, you know, these things can happen like a bolt out of the blue, don't you?'

'No, I don't. I only know that when you're married, you've made a promise, and as far as I'm concerned, you stick to it. Answer me: how long has this been going on?'

'Well, I noticed this woman at Stella and Steve's party-that must have been a year ago, we got talking…'

'But I was with you, right next to you all the time at the party!'

'No, you weren't, remember that you got us our first drinks at the bar?'

'I was just away for minutes, and you immediately started chatting up that woman? And how come that you contacted her afterwards?'

'Heather, I'm not proud of this but I was so taken by Carol that I sneaked a note into her blazer pocket with my phone number on it, asking her to contact me, and I'm afraid I've fallen in love with her since, and to my shame, I went and stayed with her when you thought I was working extra days. I was hoping to get her out of my system.'

What a lie, Heather thought and groaned.

'It was impossible, I was feeling more and more drawn to her. Honestly, I meant to talk to you openly ages ago, but I postponed it time after time. This is no infatuation, believe me, Heather, I can't be without her, and I mean to ask you for a trial separation, let's say for a year. I'm so sorry to put you in this situation, my dear. By the end of that year, it is possible that I'll have had enough of her and her girls…'

'What girls?' Heather asked though she knew about them from Stella.

'She has two daughters of twelve and fourteen.'

'And where is their father?' Heather asked.

'Oh, Carol is separated from him, and he doesn't seem to put too much effort into keeping in touch with his daughters.'

'That sounds just the perfect opportunity for you to play at being a substitute father to them, well done, Jonathan, all your problems seem to be solved now!' Heather said sarcastically.

Jonathan packed his clothes, some books, and his Country Life magazines and threw a suitcase and several bags into his car ready to leave for Carol's later the same day, partly with a bad conscience, partly relieved to have his confession behind him. Heather clung to the door handle of his car to try to stop him from leaving and sobbed and cried, making his departure very difficult for him.

For Heather, the year of the agreed separation dragged by, and Heather's feelings swung to and fro like a pendulum, hoping at times that Jonathan would have enough of life with Carol and her daughters, and sometimes convinced that she, Heather, would definitely be the one who would lose him.

At the end of the year, with Jonathan torturing her with random visits to their house, smiling and in a good mood, to collect more belongings, the moment of truth had arrived. Heather had no illusions anymore and knew in her heart of hearts that she was the biggest loser in this triangle. Jonathan told her that she as the *injured party,* should file for divorce, and he would make it easy by admitting that he was responsible for the breakdown of their marriage.

The divorce went through smoothly for Heather, not least because she had found a very competent woman solicitor who fought on her behalf. She would stay in the house. The mortgage had been paid off in less than half the time it normally took, a fact Jonathan was very proud of. This was the reward for all the extra days he had been working. Heather was to take out a loan to the tune of half the house value to pay Jonathan his share and in order to repay the loan, she would start a B&B which would also provide her with some distractions through her guests. She could also hire out her horse for some extra money to those of her guests who were experienced riders, and give riding lessons to those who were not, her own ideas which she was proud of.

It would take some time to get her B&B business off the ground through advertising and agencies. Of course, Heather knew that the very best advertising was word-of-mouth recommendations by satisfied guests.

The Cotswolds was one of the most popular tourist areas in England because of its *chocolate box* prettiness, the gently rolling hills, the old villages with their thatched cottages and flower-filled front gardens, the quaint antique shops, old-style tea places and ancient pubs. The entire area looked as though time had stood still. Heather was not worried about filling the house with guests in the summer months. If need be, and the demand was high, she would even be prepared to spend some nights on the sofa in the study so that four big bedrooms would be available for guests. *Make hay while the sun shines*, that was her motto. She was hoping to save some of her income to be able to pay the loan back in the winter months as well when bookings might well be rarer. She was not extravagant, anyway. She would not buy new clothes or shoes unless she really had to. She was a reasonable cook and could also offer three-course evening meals to guests if booked in advance so that they did not have to go out again in the evenings especially if they were travelling with children. For her dinners, she could make good use of the vegetables she grew in the garden. And there was the £ 50,000 Jonathan had given her as a lump sum.

10

He had turned up at Carol's house, with his car loaded with a suitcase and bags, even his toolbox was among his belongings. Though he had the keys to Carol's house, he had rung the bell, and when Carol answered the door with an inquisitive face, he had said dramatically, 'I'm homeless now.'

She said, 'Congratulations! How did it go?'

'I confessed our relationship to Heather, and, of course, she was distraught and tried to prevent me physically from leaving after I had packed and loaded the car.'

He omitted the fact that Heather had learnt the truth from Stella. And it slipped Carol's mind to tell Jonathan about Stella's visit. They opened a bottle of champagne to celebrate.

Life with Carol and her girls was fun, there was a lot of laughter and always something going on in the house, with the girls' school friends occasionally visiting for sleepovers or dinner parties with friends of Carol's who quickly took to Jonathan as well.

Secretly, he was waiting for Carol to announce that she had missed a period. However, this had so far not happened.

As time went on, Carol, like Heather before, started to bemoan the fact that Jonathan was away at work too often for her taste, that she missed him very much, and she occasionally asked him how he envisaged their future, hinting that she could also get divorced for them to get married. This frightened Jonathan. It would mean committing himself to Carol and also to her daughters, and he mumbled something noncommittal in reply.

Jonathan sometimes took the girls for a spin in his car, usually ending up in some café with them where he bought them cakes or ice-creams. Jonathan had just returned from working in the Netherlands for a week. On this sunny weekend afternoon in their second year together after Jonathan's divorce, he took the girls for a ride in his car. He could not help noticing that each of them was wearing a beautiful gold bracelet.

'Have you won the lottery, or how did you get hold of these charming bracelets?'

'Oh,' the girls said, 'our dad came last week and gave them to us, imagine, they are real gold, and he also took us swimming. We had such a super time together!'

Jonathan was stunned to hear that. Dante Costa, as far as he was concerned, did not really seem to exist. Carol had not said much about him, apart from the fact that they had separated two years before she met Jonathan at the party and that he seemed to have forgotten about his daughters, apart from at least reliably and voluntarily sending money for them. Only once had Jonathan seen a photo of him, a slim, tall man with black hair, worn in a ponytail, and with blue eyes, certainly a good-looking man. After their split, he had stayed in Reading where he taught at a sixth-form college. Jonathan felt somewhat alarmed that this other man had been to the home of his family when Jonathan happened to be away and must have arranged with Carol to see their daughters and take them out.

When the girls had gone to bed and he had poured a glass of wine for Carol and himself, he decided to confront her.

'I gather that you've been in touch with the father of your kids,' he said in quite an accusing tone.

'Are you going to arrest me?' retorted Carol. 'He is, after all, their father and has every right to see them, especially as he voluntarily pays maintenance for them regularly, even without a divorce. And it was him who phoned me to ask if he could take them out. It was the first time in a long time, and because the girls had been awfully upset about having been neglected by him, I was really happy for them. Of course, I welcomed his suggestion, he should do his share with the girls!'

'I saw that he bribed them by giving them bracelets,' Jonathan remarked.

Carol nearly exploded. 'Do you realise that you sound jealous, Jonathan? This is ridiculous! He's their father!'

'I wonder if he also gave a present to you,' Jonathan continued.

'Stop it this minute! I will not even answer this!' Carol shouted.

'Just remember, Carol, I never want to meet this man, so if he comes again for the girls, make sure it's when I'm not here.'

Jealousy was gnawing away at Jonathan. He decided to make some more overtures to Carol in the next few weeks, hinting at their possible marriage and pushing her to change her separation from Dante into a divorce.

In the late autumn, Jonathan learnt, again from the girls, that they had seen their father a few times in previous weeks, always when he had been working away, and to top that, that they had gone on day trips as a family at weekends. Carol had not mentioned that to him.

He felt driven to ask, 'What is going on, Carol, have you started sleeping with your husband when I'm away?' He demanded to know.

'No, I haven't,' Carol said, 'but Dante seems changed for the better, making a real effort with the girls, and he and I have managed to have some sensible talks. There's absolutely no need to feel jealous, you know!'

'Oh, I'm not jealous, Carol. I know how much you love me, and you know it's mutual. But I'd prefer to hear it from you, not the girls when he has been here.'

'I've just told you there's no reason why you should be jealous, and when the girls' father comes here for them, I just make sure he comes when you're away as you asked because you don't want to meet him. But I will not account to you for his visits! What are they to you? He's perfectly okay with the fact that you live here with us, so why can't you accept that he comes here only as their father?'

Dante's now quite regular visits to his family during Jonathan's absences made Carol realise that the feelings for him she had suppressed when they separated were surfacing again, that she and Dante were getting on better as time went on, and how lovely it was for the girls to have both parents present, how the girls seemed to sense that there was no strife between their parents anymore but harmony instead. It now increasingly got on her nerves when Jonathan flirted and joked with waitresses when they went to restaurants and turned his head to watch other women walk by, and above all, she detested his jealousy.

There's no way, I'm letting him push me towards divorcing Dante, and I really can't see myself getting married to Jonathan anymore, while the girls' dearest wish would be to live with their mother and father. Dante has changed for the better, he's so much more considerate, and I can't deny that old feelings for him have emerged again.

And so, Christmas with Jonathan was a rather strained event, especially as Dante had shyly asked if he could come around on Christmas Day and Carol, sensing that that would be the perfect scenario for some sort of showdown between Jonathan and him, had suggested a day early in the New Year instead while she and the girls would still be on holiday. Also, she knew that Jonathan had nowhere to go short of returning to Heather because Jonathan's friend Matthew who he often stayed with when working in London was away on a skiing holiday and Matt had other friends staying in his house over Christmas and New Year. There was an awkward moment when the girls asked openly in Jonathan's presence on Christmas Day why their father could not have joined them. Carol had actually made an important decision, namely, to have Dante back because he had confessed that he had fallen back in love with her and wanted to do his best for their family. Above all, his feelings were reciprocated.

Jonathan did not have to work between Christmas and early in the New Year, and Carol actually dreaded having him around for days on end. She needed to tell him of her decision to let Dante back into her life. She was hesitant and evening after evening passed without her being able to broach this difficult subject. It was the evening of New Year's Day when she finally managed to tell him.

'Jonathan, I need to tell you something. I don't know how to go about it, I guess there is simply no easy way.'

'This sounds rather doom-laden, Carol, I hope this is not about a fatal illness.'

'No, it's not. As you know, the girls and I have seen Dante quite regularly over a considerable time, and, to put it in a nutshell, Dante and I have decided to give our marriage a second chance. We've had some very constructive talks, and I feel strongly that I owe it to the girls to let them have their father back, not least because Dante and I have been able to rekindle our feelings for each other. I need to give our family this chance. It's the only decent thing to do. I'm afraid I feel that our relationship has not worked out as far as I'm concerned, and it means that I'm asking you to move out. I'm really sorry! You can stay on for a few more days but Dante and I have arranged for him to move in on 4 January.'

While listening to Carol, Jonathan had buried his head in his hands, leaning forward. He got up abruptly now, without saying anything, and went up to their bedroom. She could hear his footsteps above, the opening and closing of wardrobe doors, and after a while, he reappeared with a suitcase and several bags.

'This is it then, Carol, I know when I'm not wanted! I'll just get my toolbox from the garage, and then it's goodbye. You've been playing a double game with me, how mean of you!'

'No, I haven't. I told you that Dante came here when you weren't here, as you requested, to see the girls, and of course, I was around here as well every time he came. Your jealousy has actually been a contributory factor to the state of things now!'

Jonathan tossed the keys to the house on the coffee table in front of Carol, loaded his car and drove off.

11

Jonathan was lounging in his friend Matthew Smart's house in Denham, Buckinghamshire, a short drive out of London, with a cup of coffee in front of him, browsing through the *cars for sale* columns of *Automotive Magazine*. Whenever his job took him to the London area, he stayed with his bachelor friend Matt in whose house he had, over time, gained certain rights. He had practically taken over one of the two bedrooms, spare clothes of Jonathan's were always stored in its wardrobe, and Jonathan had a set of spare keys to Matt's house in his possession. Mind you, he remunerated Matt to the tune of £ 10 per night spent there, in cash, too! Matt was a really good mate and like Jonathan also played hockey in the company team.

Jonathan had driven down from the Cotswolds to Buckinghamshire the night before. Heather had been upset, as usual, to see him go.

It was early March, the Monday after their return from that holiday together in the sun. The first day back at work has passed quite pleasantly.

Much as he resented being back in the drizzly cold, he had been relieved to be away from Heather. Two whole weeks of almost uninterrupted togetherness had dampened his enthusiasm for his triumphant return to the fold. During the six weeks before they had departed on their holiday, his work assignments had been in a variety of places close enough to, *home*, so he had returned to Heather every night, just as she had expected. At least then he had had the comradeship and shared jokes of his work mates during the day, and the backlog of small repair jobs to be done around, *The Old Smithy*, had provided a welcome excuse to have time to himself occasionally in the evenings and during days off.

Not so on this holiday! She had always been by his side, keeping him to, the *straight and narrow*, checking if he would let his eyes roam over the female European holiday makers on the beach and in restaurants. He had been aware of missing the gamble and excitement of exchanging flirtatious glances with some beach beauties and finding out where this might lead. She had been keen to show off her conquest by holding hands with him in public at every opportunity, asking him if he really thought that she had slimmed down during her three-year ordeal, and pointing out her partly new wardrobe, fishing for compliments. Above all, she had been demanding in bed, as if wanting to make up for cold-shouldering him during the months before he had left her for Carol. He knew he had hurt her badly. It still made him feel guilty, and he had therefore been surprised by how easy it had been to slip back into her life, their former home, and the old pattern of their marriage. He had been at pains to comply with her wishes for nightly ups and downs in bed despite different levels of desire on his part.

From time to time, she had been complaining about the unreliability of her old car, so he had offered to buy her a good second-hand car after their return to England.

Buying and selling used cars was what he was good at. This had boosted their income when first married and had helped him to pay off the mortgage on their house. It was way above the standard the income from his job alone would have afforded.

He had worked out a routine which hardly ever failed: the mannerism of his first approach with a seller on the phone, the way he carried out his inspection of the car, and his own method of driving a hard bargain when it came to negotiating the price.

When selling a car, he slipped into the other role, like an actor changing costumes. He knew exactly what small talk prepared the ground for a sale, the chitchat in turn would inform him which aspects of the car to highlight to his potential buyer to make the car seem a bargain.

Heather would value the car he had promised her as a kind of new troth, particularly if the car had relatively low mileage, even if it was an older model.

He was confident to be able to find the perfect compromise, a car which would impress Heather, while not setting him back more than £ 800. Yes, that would be the limit he would set himself!

His eyes were scanning the columns more closely now as he was trying to locate an older car with low mileage.

'Austin, 1954, good condition, £ 1,000 cash, ph. Dan on 0208 598 7182.'

He must be joking to ask that sort of price for an ancient rusty tin, and no mention of the mileage which is bound to be astronomical!

Daihatsu Charade, 86, 5 speed, met. Blue, no rust, 60.000 m, £ 3,500, ph. Paul on 0208 360 0994.

Nope, I'll give that one a miss.

Fiat Strada, 84, 30,000 m, £ 3,800, ph. 0207 754 3348.

Too pricey, I won't be able to get that one down to £ 800!

Ford Escort, 1984, 27,000 m, complete service record, £ 2,000, ph. 0208 759 2493.

Sounds interesting,' Jonathan mused. 'I'll give this number a ring. That one's much more likely.

He dialled the number which he recognised as a Chiswick one.

Handy! It will only be a ten-minute drive from the office in Acton.

'Hello,' a warm female voice said at the other end.

'Hi, I'm phoning about the car. Is it still available?'

'Yes, it is, actually.'

The voice had the quality of an intriguingly foreign accent to it.

'May I ask where you're from?'

'I'm from Belgium originally.'

'How interesting! I'm a quarter French myself. Has there been much interest in the car?'

'Yes, I've had people phone up about it, and a couple of them are coming here the day after tomorrow to look at it.'

'And you have a complete service record?'

'Yes, certainly.'

'I'd like to come to look at the car. When would be convenient?'

'How about tomorrow?'

'Okay, let me see, would 3:30 suit you tomorrow afternoon?'

'Fine.'

'Can I have the address, please, then?'

'Oh, it's 16, Fairlawn Crescent. I'd better explain how to get here from Chiswick Park tube station.'

'Don't worry. I'll be coming by car. I'll find my way.'

'Okay, really? Can I have your name, please?'

'It's Mr Shilling.'

'See you tomorrow, then.'

'Yes, bye!'

12

Nicola Hyatt was feeling quite upset. It was the first Monday in March. She had been a part-time teacher of adult immigrants in West London for the last five years.

Perhaps it was because she was still shaken from an extraordinary experience when teaching that morning. She was reading a story with a man from Sri Lanka while the rest of her students had some written work to do. They came across the word, *sand* in the text, and Nicola asked him if he knew what that meant. He shook his head, so Nicola took a pencil and paper and drew a beach with waves and palm trees and stabbed her pencil at the paper countless times to make dots to represent, *sand*, then asked the man again, and again, to her disbelief, he shook his head. She then got out her imaginary spade and started digging up the classroom floor, with all the students staring at this crazy teacher. Again, her student shook his head and she vowed that she'd bring in a bag of sand the next day if it was the last thing she ever taught!

During the break, her colleague Rose told her that in some countries shaking your head means, *yes*, and nodding means, *no*. So, this meant her student understood the word straightaway, and she made a right fool of herself! Body language does not mean the same worldwide, she should have thought of that.

She paced up and down in her semi-detached house in typical London suburban style from the late 1930s and caught sight of the Ford Escort, which had been parked in the drive since November. The sight of it made her depressed, more than she could say. She had bought the Ford Escort for her older son Zac. He was twenty-one and had constantly been borrowing her own car. Since Zac started his university course in Central London, this second car had become redundant. Even the university lecturers found it difficult to park their cars in the tiny Uni car park, let alone the nerve-racking drive into Central London. Nicola had advertised the car regularly and there had not even been a phone enquiry. With every passing day, the car was losing in value, what with getting older and being exposed to the danger of rusting.

The car had probably been the worst investment of her life. It cost her close to £ 4,000 to buy despite being second-hand, and a few weeks after the purchase it needed major repairs, which cost another £ 600. And her money certainly did not grow on trees. Since her divorce ten years ago, she had been responsible for bringing up her two sons, Zac and his younger brother Ben, now nineteen, on her own. Her ex had been either unemployed or, when working, had not paid the maintenance for the boys. So, Nicola had used her teacher training as an English teacher from her home country Belgium to run residential English courses in her house for continental teenagers during their holidays at Easter and in the summer to make ends meet. Then, at the end of a year back at college, she had gained a postgraduate diploma in her field and had secured her present 15-hour-a-week post. She taught her private courses at home when she herself was on holiday from college over Easter and in the summer. It worked out perfectly.

Nicola was rummaging in her school bag to search for teaching materials when the phone rang. She was relieved to get a break from her search, grateful, in fact, to whoever was interrupting her by phoning.

She was thrilled to hear a man at the other end of the phone who seemed genuinely interested in the car. She was so keen to be rid of it that she lied when he asked her if there had been interest from others in the car.

The inspection arranged for the following afternoon prompted her to give the car its first thorough wash in four months.

13

During the next morning's teaching, Nicola started thinking about how important it was to her to sell the car to, *what was his name again? Oh, yes, Mr Shilling*, this afternoon.

It occurred to her that both her sons would still be away at that time of day, and, judging by the newspaper reports, it was not advisable to ask an unknown man into your house when you were a female alone, least of all in London.

Nicola decided to ask her next-door neighbour a favour. Jane worked from home. She was to ring her doorbell at 3:45 pm, about a quarter of an hour after Mr Shilling should have arrived. If Nicola then asked Jane in, it would mean that she did not feel safe in Mr Shilling's presence.

Later, at home, while Nicola collected the service records for the car together, she changed her mind. She would plug the radio in upstairs.

Radio 3 had plenty of talk programmes, and if she left the radio on at a muttering level, anyone would think that there were people talking upstairs or at least that someone upstairs was listening to the radio. *A clever deterrent!* she thought.

Nicola also decided to keep her black skirt and smart black and white wool jacket from the teaching session on, plus her high-heeled black shoes, for the proper saleswoman look, rather than slipping into a pair of jeans and a t-shirt.

Punctually, at 3:30 pm, the doorbell rang. Nicola had put the car papers on the worktop in her kitchen cum breakfast room. She walked to her front door and opened it. Opposite her stood a tall, burly man with a charming smile on his tanned face, his head tilted at an angle while he introduced himself in a soft voice. He was casually dressed in corduroy jeans, a cotton polo neck pullover and a brown leather jacket.

Nicola smiled back, greeted him and led him to the car. She unlocked the doors and the boot, opened the bonnet and hoped for the best. She was surprised to see Mr Shilling start a thorough check. He seemed to know what he was looking for when he scratched the inside metal of the boot. Not long after, he had crawled underneath the car, with his body just protruding from the waist down. Nicola noticed that he was wearing aubergine-coloured underpants.

It was a really cold day, like yesterday, when she washed the car. Mr Shilling now asked Nicola if he could take the car for a trial run. It appeared a good sign to her, so she eagerly agreed.

Embarrassing for her, it was at this point that Mr Shilling noticed a flat tyre. She regretted having told him that there had been plenty of interest in the car, for he surely had to see that it had been a while since it had last been driven.

Mr Shilling strolled over to his car, a Mercedes. Unusually, it was bright orange. He got out a tyre pump and had pumped up the flat tyre in no time. Still, there was no way she would allow him to drive off in the car for the test drive, so she sat down next to him in the passenger seat while he drove along her road and round the corner, not a long drive by any means but gentlemanly Mr Shilling had made sure her seat belt was fastened.

'By the way, my name is Jonathan,' he said during the short drive. Nicola reciprocated by giving her first name.

Getting out of the car again in front of Nicola's house, he said, 'You're so smartly dressed, are you going somewhere special?'

Nicola started telling him about her teaching session that morning.

She decided on the spur of the moment that it was far too cold a day not to invite Jonathan in for a cup of coffee to talk business, because, surely, this was the next step. He would want to buy the car, wouldn't he?

Jonathan sat down at the large oak table in Nicola's kitchen and took off his heavy jacket while Nicola busied herself with the coffee machine, cups, saucers, and milk jug…When she turned to sit down at the table, she was not surprised to see confirmation of Jonathan's bulging stomach which had been a mere suggestion under the jacket. Hidden under the jacket was also his workplace ID. Nicola checked his name and hoped he did not notice. Upstairs, the radio was murmuring.

'How come you're a quarter French?' she made conversation while the coffee machine hissed.

'My mother is half-French through her father but grew up in England.'

'Your French must be pretty good,' Nicola continued.

'I used to spend quite a few summers with my French relatives near Tours, but I'm afraid I only speak a few words in French so won't be able to have a conversation with you in your mother tongue. They were all so keen on practising their English on me!'

'My mother tongue isn't French but Flemish. You know, Belgium is bi-lingual, but of course, I learnt French at school and am quite fluent in it.'

The coffee was ready to be poured. After a couple of sips, Jonathan complimented Nicola on the excellent aroma of her coffee. Nicola was pleased about the compliment and at the same time, she was astonished that she was, it being such a platitude.

'Why do you want another car? The orange car you came in is yours, isn't it?' Nicola wanted to know.

'I'm buying this car for my ex-wife,' Jonathan explained.

Nicola thought that this must be part of the divorce settlement.

She wanted to change the subject and asked, 'Have you just come back from a skiing holiday?' looking into Jonathan's tanned face.

'No, I've just been to the Dominican Republic for a couple of weeks. It's great to get the sun on your back during the English winter and spend time on the beach. Mind you, people there are unbelievably prudish, there wasn't a single topless woman to be seen on the beach.' He smiled suggestively at Nicola who suddenly wondered if she should not have asked Jane to ring her doorbell, after all.

Nicola did not want to dwell on this topic, so told Jonathan why she wanted to sell her car and mentioned it was for her older son who now used the tube to get to university.

'How long have you been living in England for?'

It was Jonathan's turn to be inquisitive.

'For nearly twenty-five years now, and the last sixteen here in Chiswick.'

'I bet your hubby works for an airline, with Heathrow so close,' Jonathan probed, and Nicola was torn between pretending she was married or owning up to her divorced status.

She remembered that Jonathan had just mentioned an ex-wife, so she decided to be honest, but she was not charmed by Jonathan's roundabout way of extracting the information.

What a tired ploy, she thought.

'I'm feeling quite sorry for myself at the moment,' Jonathan told her next, hinting at a recent break-up in a relationship by which he might or might not refer to his marriage.

'Do you live in London?' Nicola asked him.

'Well, yes and no. When I work in or near London, I stay with a friend and colleague in Denham, not far out of London. My ex-wife is still in the house we lived in together and runs it as a B&B. It's a listed building from the late 18th century. It was the village smithy in Milton-under-Wychwood in the Cotswolds. The old anvil is still there but in an outbuilding.'

'How fascinating,' Nicola commented.

The really difficult thing now was to bring the conversation around to talking business. There seemed no other way but a sudden change of topic.

'Are you going to make me an offer for the car?' Nicola asked outright.

Jonathan gave her a run-down of all the places where he noticed rust and how he would have to spend at least £ 200 to have that seen to. Nicola pointed out the low mileage and showed Jonathan the regular service records.

'Well, taking everything into account, I'm prepared to offer you £ 800 for it.'

Jonathan was driving a hard bargain. Nicola's heart sank.

'I'm asking £ 2,000, just half of what I paid myself for the car.'

'No one will pay £ 2,000 for a 1984 Ford Escort, I can guarantee that, so I'm afraid I will have to keep to my offer.'

Nicola knew this was the crunch point. If she insisted on £ 2,000, her only potential buyer would get up and go. He seemed to know about the car market, which she did not. On the other hand, selling the car for £ 2, 000 would already have meant a great concession, and she could not seriously consider only £ 800 for it.

'I'll take £ 1,000,' she announced in a voice which she hoped did not show how shaken she was.

Jonathan hesitated, then agreed.

'Okay, but I only have £ 800 in cash on me. I've got to go to a cash machine.' He was getting up from the table. 'I won't be long.'

While Nicola cleared away the cups, she was quite pleased with her small triumph. 'He was only prepared to spend £ 800 and is now fetching another £ 200 to buy the car!' She would finally be rid of it!

I can't wait to tell the boys, she thought.

On his return, Jonathan made her count all the money. Nicola handed over the car documents.

Then Jonathan said, 'I work at our London office quite regularly, while I stay with my friend Matthew in Denham. I wonder if you'd like to join me at your corner pub for a drink at lunchtime sometime.'

Nicola did not want to commit herself.

'Well, you've got my phone number. You could call me, and I'll tell you then. How are you going to take the car? It hasn't got a road licence at the moment.'

'I'll leave it in your drive and just take the keys for now. I'll organise the licence and collect the car tomorrow if I may.'

'It's yours now,' Nicola answered and thought, *to be exact, it's your ex-wife's.*

Nicola saw Jonathan to the door to say goodbye. He took her hand and gave her a mock hand kiss.

Nicola withdrew her hand, embarrassed, and said, 'What did you do that for? Is that the quarter Frenchman in you?'

Jonathan laughed and explained that he was romantic as he was a Piscean. Nicola wanted to know when his birthday was.

'February 22nd,' Jonathan answered.

'But that's my eldest son's birthday, too!' she commented excitedly. 'What a coincidence! By the way, I'm a Piscean, too.'

'When's your birthday, then?' Jonathan wanted to know now.

'Not till mid-March,' Nicola mumbled modestly. After all, it was in just over two weeks' time.

That evening, Nicola told her sons the great news, 'Guess what! I sold the car this afternoon.'

'That's brilliant news, Mum, but how come the car is still in the drive?' Ben asked.

Nicola explained and told the boys every detail of her conversation with Jonathan Shilling.

'Be careful, Mum,' they both said, 'he's after you.'

'Don't worry about me,' Nicola said to her sons who were as protective as parents.

That evening, Jonathan phoned Heather to tell her about her new car. Heather was so pleased. Jonathan would drive the car to her when his present work assignment had finished. It meant waiting for a few days.

The next day, Nicola had a new adult student in her class, a young woman from India who came with her 2-month-old baby. While copying words from the board, she was breastfeeding her baby.

I hope the baby will imbibe some English with his mother's milk, she thought.

When she returned from teaching, the car had gone from the drive. Zac told her that he met Jonathan when he came to collect the car and handed her a note Jonathan had left for her.

'He's even left a love letter, Mum,' Zac commented.

C/o M. Smart
32, Church Lane
Denham
Bucks.
Tel. 01895 274963

Dear Nicola,

I'm sorry you were out when I called to collect the car. You forgot to write me a receipt for the money I paid, so could you please send it to me at the above address?

Thanks in advance,

Jonathan.

Nicola sat down straightaway, wrote the receipt for Mr Shilling and posted it in the letterbox around the corner from her house.

14

Nicola knew that that was that, meaning the transaction was over now. She wouldn't have any more dealings with Mr Jonathan Shilling. Then she remembered his invitation to join him for a lunchtime drink one day at her corner pub.

Oh, men say a lot of things, and, anyway, she didn't really fancy him, with his potbelly. And why did he tell her so much about himself? That's odd,' she mused, 'why should a person buying a car from me impart so much information about himself? Christ, I even know about his French grandfather! How ridiculous! He won't ring me again, that's for sure, though he's made sure now that I've got his landline number, too, at his friend's! As if I would chase a man, least of all one whose friend might take the call. How embarrassing it would be to ask for Mr Shilling on the phone, and this friend would overhear our conversation...

Her thoughts drifted away while she was staring out of her kitchen window into the garden. Slowly the leaves outside came into focus again, and Nicola scolded herself.

The team, teaching English as a Second Language to Adult Immigrants, consisted of three women teachers. They reported to their team leader, Richard. They shared an unusual classroom, which was the Council Chamber of the local Town Hall. There was only one movable board to write on, so every morning, the three teachers negotiated who could have the board before or after the break, and the third teacher took her break at a different time so she could use the board while the other two teachers relaxed with a coffee mid-morning. If a teacher needed her students to copy something down but had not got the board, she held up large pieces of sugar paper until her arms tired.

Third World conditions for Third World people, Nicola thought with a grudge.

The students, male and female, were from India, Pakistan, Sri Lanka, Afghanistan, Iraq and Iran and ranged in age from teenage to 80. The lessons were free. *This was not necessarily a good thing*, Nicola thought. Some students came only for a single time, others attended regularly for months on end and then stayed away for two or three weeks. If the students had to pay a modest sum each term, they would probably take the classes more seriously.

Most of the students were not well-versed in the Latin script, and some of the men, especially those from a war zone, were more skilled at taking a rifle apart and assembling it again than holding a pencil to write with. It was difficult for all the students to focus on their teacher all the time with another two classes going on simultaneously in the same room.

A few days later, during the morning break, while Rose and Nicola were waiting for the water to boil, Nicola asked Rose, 'What about your two new students? I noticed them this morning, that young woman and an elderly man with a turban and long white beard.'

'Oh, that older man is the girl's father, and he wants to make sure that his unmarried daughter doesn't sit next to a man, he himself doesn't want any English lessons,' Rose explained.

While stirring her coffee and settling down to the daily chat with her colleague Rose, the sale of the car and Mr Jonathan Shilling came to mind, and Nicola told Rose the amusing story of how they met. When she had finished, Rose commented, 'I'm convinced that you have an admirer.' Nicola laughed it off. It did sound absurd.

Days went by and Nicola forgot Jonathan Shilling. Then, ten days after the sale of the car, it was a Saturday afternoon, the phone rang.

'Hello?'

'Oh, hello there, is that Nicola?'

'Yes.'

'It's Jonathan Shilling here. How are you?'

'I'm fine, thanks.'

'I'm calling you from the BBC lorry. We're recording a match this afternoon. I'm just wondering if you'd like to go to a party with me tonight.'

'I'm already going out to the theatre tonight, and then to a party, no, I can't.'

'What a pity! Well, I'll ring you again soon, if I may.'

'Okay, goodbye then.'

Nicola was quite flustered and flattered though he had proved her wrong with what she said about men's promises. Even if it hadn't been true about going out tonight, she would not have gone out with him at such short notice!

After the weekend, Jonathan rang her up again.

'Hello, Nicola, Jonathan here again. How are you? What about us going to your corner pub together on Wednesday for a drink? Can you make 7:30? I'll collect you in my car, see you then!' And he hung up before she could reply or object.

Nicola's thoughts circled about the big difference between meeting Jonathan at lunchtime and in the evening. All sorts of dangers lurked around such an evening date, like: should she say goodbye in his car in front of her house after he had driven her back? What form would this goodbye take, or should she ask him in for a cup of coffee? This cup of coffee would be interpreted as quite a different invitation, or rather, misinterpreted. It was all so complicated; on the other hand, it was quite exciting.

On Wednesday, Jonathan was ten minutes early when he rang the doorbell. How impolite to be early, Nicola registered. Nicola threw her coat over, then dashed out. Jonathan opened and closed her car door for her. How attentive, how polite, Nicola registered. The drive was short, they were early enough to get a small table in the room with a fire in the fireplace. It was cosy. Now that they were in the light, subdued as it was, Nicola studied Jonathan. He was wearing light grey corduroy jeans and a soft woollen-polo neck sweater in the same colour which was wide enough to hide his belly. His broad open face smiled at her, dimples appeared on his cheeks and he asked her what he could get for her. Nicola fancied a glass of dry white wine, and Jonathan disappeared to the bar in the room next door.

To her amazement, he returned with a whole bottle of the finest French white wine and two glasses. Conversation flowed easily, he asked her about her teaching situation, and talked about his job, she told him that she had just discovered that one of her older women among her students did not know her date of birth.

'That's really handy, isn't it? She can always claim that she's ten years younger than she really is.' He laughed.

'But she doesn't know how old she really is,' Nicola commented, rolling her eyes and adding, 'not knowing your date of birth can have serious implications, it's not all that funny.'

He could be quite amusing. He seemed to like puns. He said that if he ran a double-glazing company, he'd call it, *Pane in the Glass*.

Ouch, Nicola thought but could not help laughing.

He looked pensive for a short while, then came out with his idea for a hair salon, *Barber Black Sheep*. They laughed, and their hands touched on the small table between them.

Jonathan always stayed with his friend Matthew when he worked in or around London and there he would head after their evening together. He also travelled a lot around the country in the course of his work and sometimes had to go abroad to record sports matches. Jonathan also said that the car was running very well.

He must have seen his ex-wife to deliver the car to her, then, Nicola thought, and said, 'I'm glad to hear that.'

Time passed swiftly and they got up when, the *last orders*, bell was rung. They held hands for the hundred yards to where Jonathan's car was parked. He unlocked Nicola's door first, took her into his arms and kissed her gently, closed the door and sat down beside her.

Before Nicola had had time to argue the case for or against the invitation to a cup of coffee, they were back outside her house, and she heard herself ask, 'Would you like to come in for a cup of coffee?'

He kept her company in the kitchen while she busied herself making the coffee. He gallantly carried the tray through to the sitting room.

Next to each other on the sofa, they soon lay in each other's arms. Jonathan wanted to fondle Nicola's breasts and make love to her. But Nicola was adamant on not to go that far on a first date.

He tore himself away, it was well after midnight and he mumbled something about not making his friend Matthew suspicious. They arranged to meet again on Sunday afternoon.

15

He collected her from her house, and they drove off in his car. 'Where are you taking me?' she asked.

'I'm whisking you away to the countryside for a walk,' he announced.

It was indeed a pleasant spring day. Though crisp, it was sunny. There was a lock on the canal near Denham in Buckinghamshire. To get there, you crossed a private golf course and a couple of meadows with cows on them from Denham village. As they approached the lock, they could see one of the narrow canal boats in it and watch the water level go up and down, the gates open again and the boat continuing on its way. It was a pretty boat, painted quite patriotically in red, white and blue, with a painted tin jug and several flowerpots on the deck. The tow path was deserted, they were the only walkers. Nicola felt a trifle nervous. Could she trust him, or not? It was a bit late to ask this question.

She was trying to make conversation.

'You know, our team leader advised us not to refer to the board in the class as blackboard, even though it's black.'

'Oh my goodness, I can't believe that! It's typical of a Labour Council falling over backwards to avoid accusations of racism! The next thing we'll know is that we'll all have to call black coffee "coffee without milk", and white coffee "coffee with milk".'

Well, Nicola thought, *how come I have this hunch that he votes Conservative,* but she did not reply.

He had put his arm around her shoulder, and they walked along the canal, crossed several bridges and eventually reached another lock with a lock keeper's cottage where cream teas were on offer. Jonathan ordered and joked with the lockkeeper's wife. They indulged in their tea. There was so much cream, Nicola got some on her fingers. Jonathan licked the cream off. Just then, his phone rang, and Nicola could overhear the conversation. There was a woman on the other end.

'The tap in the kitchen is dripping. When can you come to see to it?'

'Let me see, at the earliest in mid-week when I have my next free day.'

'Where are you now?'

'I'm at the office in Acton, and I can't speak for long. So, see you probably on Wednesday! Bye.'

Nicola was flabbergasted at the lie he'd just uttered. Who did he feel he needed to mislead? She definitely wanted to know.

'Do you have an extra job as a plumber and are you at your clients' beck and call?' she asked him.

He took a moment to answer and was obviously embarrassed at having been caught lying so obviously.

'Oh, how shall I put it? I don't blame you for being puzzled but that was my ex-wife who still relies on me to fix little jobs in the house. I don't want to make her jealous unnecessarily, you know. She takes everything so much to heart. I think she might have expected me with her today…'

'But she's not your wife, she's your ex-wife, you told me, and that should mean that jealousy doesn't come into it now that you're divorced and free!' Nicola exclaimed.

'How long have you been divorced?'

'For two years, and before that, we were separated for a year,' he said. 'I still go to see her from time to time. She was shattered when I left her, you must understand.'

'It's quite a distance to travel to fix a tap,' Nicola remarked.

She was very upset. Jonathan did not seem as free as she thought.

There is no way I'm ever going to tell Nicola that Heather and I have recently resumed our marriage despite staying divorced, he swore to himself. *Ignorance is bliss, isn't it?*

And this worked two ways as it concerned Heather as well with regard to Nicola.

The atmosphere was dampened, however, and they walked back to the car mostly in silence. Nicola made conversation by asking him again how, *her*, car was running. He assured her that it was running really well and that his ex-wife was pleased to hear that the car had a woman owner before her.

So, Nicola thought, *he must have mentioned to his ex-wife who he bought the car from.*

She did not ask him in when he stopped the car in front of her house.

'I'll phone you, Nicola. See you really soon, I hope!'

Nicola mumbled, 'Yes, do hope!'

16

Three days after their Sunday outing along the canal, Jonathan did drive up to the Cotswolds, reluctantly though, to fix that dripping tap in the kitchen of their house, and anyway, he was due to stay at home with Heather for a few days. Heather seemed to be at her wit's end.

'I discovered the drip on Sunday, and I had to let the phone ring for ages before you picked it up, Jonathan!'

'Yes, Heather,' he said in an irritated voice, 'remember what I told you? I was working in the Acton office, and I can't just answer the phone in the middle of my work at any given time. You've got to understand this! It might be better if I ring you once a day, or even twice a day, rather than you having to risk interrupting me. My boss gets really nerved by that sort of thing. Also, from that distance, I can't repair the tap, don't you see?'

That repeated lie about working in Acton flashed out of his mouth with such ease, it astonished him. He congratulated himself on the ploy of him ringing her when away, rather than her ringing him. It would guarantee peace and quiet when he was with Nicola, or so he hoped. If Nicola wanted to ever see him again, that was.

She had started to find Jonathan amusing, entertaining and quite attractive as a person. He had also been generous and seemed to have a positive outlook on life. During the next few phone calls from Jonathan, she was off-hand and did not accept any of his invitations to go to the cinema, out for a meal, for a walk, or to the theatre.

Then the flowers started to arrive, interspersed with postcards from places where he was working. Invariably, the flowers were red roses, big bunches of them.

Zac and Ben made their comments, 'Mum, he really wants you, doesn't he?'

'Give him a chance, we don't mind. He seems really nice.'

What on earth are those flowers and postcards supposed to mean? Nicola thought, though the answer was plain to her.

He was keen on her, and he was persistent, that was for sure. The colour postcards were from Edinburgh, Manchester, Norwich, Bristol and Amsterdam, the messages were short and to the point, like *Missing you, Wish you were here, Hoping to see you soon, Thinking of you all the time.* All the cards were signed with, *All my love, J* or *Fondest love, J.*

Nicola was slightly annoyed by the flowers and postcards because they were intended to put pressure on her, she could clearly see that, and also a little pleased to be courted, or what is the dated word, *wooed.*

A month had passed since their walk along the canal and the interruption of the phone call from the ex-wife which showed Jonathan up as a liar. Could he simply be a kind person who still helped his ex-partner? That would be another way of seeing the incident though the obvious lie still jarred. Perhaps enough time had passed to agree to another meeting with Jonathan to observe and assess him. When he next phoned, he invited her to see, *the Mousetrap*, by Agatha Christie in the theatre. It was one of the longest-running plays ever, something like over forty-two years. It was a chance to dress up. They had excellent seats, and drinks in the interval, just as well as the play was somewhat dusty and needed rinsing. After the play, Jonathan's phone remained switched off, and he invited Nicola to dinner and dance at Samantha's nightclub on Burlington Street. Being there felt grand. There was no shortage of topics to talk about, Jonathan was amusing when talking about working in all the places he sent postcards from, and they laughed frequently. The dinner was superb, the atmosphere glamorous, the lighting very subtle, the band wonderful, and the wine excellent. What was the word again? Yes. Nicola felt, *wooed*. When they danced, she felt secure in Jonathan's arms, which gripped her tightly. Jonathan hailed a black cab when they left the club, and Nicola invited him into her house in Chiswick. They spent their first intoxicating night together. This time, there was no mention on Jonathan's part that he did not want to make his friend Matthew in Denham suspicious. It felt wonderful to wake up next to each other.

'We should do this again,' Jonathan said. Nicola smiled in response.

17

The months went by, and Nicola was definitely in love with Jonathan. She thought it was mutual. She loved his company and his cheerful ways. He had the gift to make her laugh, which woman would not like that? They were now together once or twice a week on those occasions when Jonathan had to work in or near London, either at Nicola's house or at Matt's. So far, there had been no more emergency calls about dripping taps. On the contrary, Jonathan tended to keep his mobile switched off when they were together, and together they were, especially at night. When Jonathan had to work further afield or abroad, Nicola missed him sorely, and he phoned her regularly.

What she did not know was that six months after his return to Heather and the resumption of their *marriage*, he had reluctantly repaid the loan Heather had taken out from the bank, so Heather was free from the monthly repayments. They had been to see a solicitor, and both names were again on the deeds of the house. For Heather, this was the triumph she had been dreaming of. Their relationship was obviously working, otherwise, Jonathan would not have agreed to that, would he? If only he was not away from home so often and for such long stretches of time!

Nicola was expecting him at her house in the spring of the second year of their *acquaintance*, to put it coyly, to stay the night when she received a phone call from Jonathan.

'Where are you, Jonathan, can I expect you as arranged a bit later?' she asked, sensing that something out of the ordinary had happened as he only phoned if he needed to cancel a visit.

'You won't believe it, Nicola, but I'm phoning you from Kingston Hospital.'

'Oh, no, Jonathan, what has happened? Are you okay?'

'Yes, I'm still alive but I've broken my wrist playing hockey in the company team. It's a complicated fracture, and I'm supposed to have a little operation tomorrow morning to set the bones and put the wrist in plaster. They'll keep me in until the day after tomorrow, but you can visit me here tomorrow afternoon, say at 4 pm?'

'I'll definitely do that. Are you in a lot of pain, darling?'

'No, my love, they've given me some strong painkillers. So, see you tomorrow, then?'

'Just give me the name of your ward.'

Nicola was upset about Jonathan's fracture but there was a glimmer of hope: he would not be able to drive, surely, so that could mean he would be staying with her for an extended period.

The next afternoon, she could not wait to see him and arrived at the hospital as early as 3:30 pm. She found his ward quite easily, and on looking into the room through the open door, saw a smart-looking woman bending over a patient and kissing him. On straightening up, she realised with a shock that the patient was Jonathan. Who on earth was this woman? Surely not his sister who lived in Shrewsbury! Just then, a nurse asked her which patient she was here to visit, and she said Jonathan's name.

'Oh, he is very popular with the ladies,' the nurse said.

Nicola was shaken, stepped aside and walked to the end of the corridor. She was quite sure that Jonathan had not seen her stand in the open door of his ward. At the end of the corridor was a ladies' toilet. She stepped in, locked herself in a cubicle and let her tears flow. She hadn't got enough tissues on her so had to use some loo paper to stem the flow. A look at her watch told her she had twenty more minutes before Jonathan expected her. What to do? Should she follow her head or her heart? Her head told her to leave the hospital and never to have anything to do with Jonathan again. Her heart, however, demanded an explanation of what she had just witnessed, otherwise, her thoughts would forever be circling around this episode. She took a look in the mirror. Her eyes were reddened and swollen from crying. She felt overwhelmingly strongly that it was too late. This did not refer to the time on her watch but to her relationship with Jonathan. She was deeply in love with him and could not let him go. She put some cold water on her face, then made it up again. She would go and see Jonathan. Close to 4 o'clock she entered his ward. His visitor had gone, which was probably why he had given her a time to visit him. He would be sure this female would have gone by then.

'Hello, darling, how are you feeling?' she said while bending down to kiss him.

He looked at her askance, 'Have you been crying, Nicola? What on earth is the matter?'

Nicola blushed and did not want the other patients on the ward to overhear their conversation, so she whispered, 'I thought I saw a woman visitor by your bed a short time ago when I passed the door to your ward. Who is she?'

Jonathan was obviously not prepared for this question and fumbled in the drawer of his bedside table to win some time.

'Oh, that was an old friend of mine. I phoned her from here, and she happened to be on the train into Paddington from where she lives for a day out in London, and she kindly offered to cheer me up for half an hour.'

'That's a hell of a coincidence, I must say! Is she an old flame, Jonathan, and have you just lit it again? So, you phone her up from time to time. Do you go to see her, too? I know you keep on seeing your ex-wife, too, and I don't want to be part of your harem!'

'Calm down, Nicola, it really is not as bad as it must appear to you. Her name is Carol, and I was living with her for quite some time, but she is now reunited with her husband.'

Nicola, with a woman's intuition, asked if she was the reason for Jonathan's divorce from his wife, and he nodded.

'I saw her kiss you as I was walking past the door,' Nicola commented in a shaky voice.

'Look, Nicola, that doesn't mean a thing. We're not together anymore. She's just an old friend, and what's a kiss between old friends?'

Nicola stayed silent, then asked, 'You won't be able to drive for a while, and I take it for granted that I'll collect you from the hospital the day after tomorrow, and that you'll be staying with me until you can go to work again.'

'That's very kind of you, Nicola, to want to collect me by car. Thank you. A broken wrist won't be accepted as a reason not to turn up for work. From your place, I could easily take the tube to the office where I can at least do some paperwork. The hand I write with is okay.'

Nicola envisaged a few weeks with Jonathan living with her and was content. Another kiss from another female, and she was gone.

18

Jonathan had phoned Heather as soon as he had arrived at the hospital. She was predictably upset and immediately wanted to drive to Kingston to be with him. But she had B&B guests staying at *The Old Smithy*, and could not get away, which prompted a sigh of relief from Jonathan. She was all set on collecting him a couple of days later, though, after his operation and his reply had been non-committal,

'Let's see how it goes, Heather, and then we'll talk some more.'

In the late afternoon of the next day, the doorbell rang at *The Old Smithy*. This was the time of day when Heather often managed to fill the remaining bedrooms of the B&B with a particular kind of tourist, in the summer months, anyway. There were those who painstakingly planned and pre-booked everything from accommodation to activities and museum visits when they went on a trip, and there were those who liked leaving things to chance and had learnt to trust that they would always somehow find somewhere to sleep. It was this latter kind of tourist who often knocked on Heather's door in the late afternoon and asked if there was a room available and if there was, she usually delighted them by asking if they would like a three-course dinner as well. If she was fully booked, she offered to phone a neighbour who also ran a B&B in the village to ask if she could accommodate them. They had a reciprocal system that way which worked well.

Heather rushed to the door, tidying her hair with her hands, and was astonished to see Stella standing there. She was still grateful to Stella for having told her the hard truth of Jonathan's affair with Carol all that time ago. It had given Heather a choice over her own life. Yes, it had led to her divorce from Jonathan but at least neither she nor he were living a lie. Like in a fairy tale, the outcome had been a happy ending: Jonathan had returned to her for good, she had been able to pay back the loan to the bank as Jonathan had returned the money for his share of the house to her, and now she was earning money in the most pleasant way she could imagine, from her own home.

'How lovely to see you, Stella,' she exclaimed, 'come in!'

'I've been to Burford and thought I'd drop in to see how you are, Heather. We're both so busy and haven't seen much of each other for a while. I should have phoned but I decided on the spur of the moment, so here I am! Is Jonathan in?'

Stella was not keen on seeing him as he had been bearing her a grudge ever since she told Heather of his affair.

'No, he's not. Do you know what's happened? He phoned me from Kingston Hospital yesterday. He's broken his wrist playing hockey! He's had an operation this morning to set his wrist. He can leave the hospital tomorrow. Of course, I want to collect him and take him here to recuperate and look after him but for whatever reason, he doesn't seem so keen. I do wonder, why. Tea, coffee? Let me put the kettle on.'

'Where does he stay when he is working in or near London, Heather?'

'He's got a really nice colleague, Matthew, who has a house in Denham quite near London where Jonathan more or less occupies one of the two bedrooms. I'm a bit worried because Jonathan has forbidden me to phone him during the day. He says his boss does not like his employees to have private phone conversations when they are supposed to be working, and he has really irregular working hours. So, he phones me, sometimes during his lunch break and mostly in the evening, and after he phones me, he often switches off his phone. I'm not comfortable with the fact that my hands are tied, and he completely controls our contact when he's away. Stella, do tell me the truth, do you think he's still seeing Carol, or am I hyper-sensitive?'

'What you're saying sounds a bit fishy to me as if he's hiding something, to be honest. But I can assure you that Carol is really happy with the return of her husband and would not contemplate for a minute to risk her marriage and family harmony by taking up with Jonathan again, believe me.'

'Okay, that's a relief to know. But the other day when he was here with me, he got a phone call on his mobile, left the room and closed the door, which always makes me suspicious. So, I stood on the other side of the door and could make out the name "Nicola." I wonder if that's someone at work, I just wouldn't know. I'm hesitant to ask Jonathan outright if something is going on. He might be totally innocent, Stella, and he promised to me to be completely faithful when I took him back. What would you do?'

Stella sat and thought for a moment, then said, 'My mother used to say, "Trust is great, but a check-up is better".'

'There is no easy way about it. If you want clarity, you will either have to ask Jonathan, mind you, he might not tell you the truth when he answers, or you can employ a private investigator who will soon come up with the truth. Think about it, Heather, I would!'

'Oh, Stella, I'd feel so shabby spying on Jonathan. But, on the other hand, I feel really vulnerable and need to know what is, or is not, going on. Thanks for your tip. I'll definitely think about it, Stella.'

19

That night in the hospital, Jonathan was lying there, thinking,

I deceived Heather with Carol for nearly a year, and then I was found out because I did not take my chance to own up. And now I've been deceiving Heather with Nicola for about the same length of time. This really must make me a despicable person, and I almost wonder if I deceive myself in a way. I certainly don't like all these complications I have to deal with, these mental acrobatic acts of not letting one woman know what I'm doing with the other, but I just can't leave things alone.

He was thinking as well about how on earth he could get out of this present predicament. Of course, he had also phoned Heather who was beside herself at the news and wanted Jonathan home until his wrist had mended. She, too, had offered to collect him from the hospital all the way from the Cotswolds and was looking forward to nursing him like a baby. He would have to explain to her that he was not an invalid and would continue to work at the Acton office though, he would not be able to travel to sporting events where he needed both hands for the recording apparatus. This tug of war between Nicola and Heather was enough aggravation to make him temporarily wish he was a one-woman man. The safest thing would be to stay with Matthew in Denham for a while, a neutral haven. It was Matthew who, a player in his hockey team, had taken him to hospital. Matt was not married, nor did he have a girlfriend at the moment, and Jonathan thought he had neglected his friend for too long as it was. In fact, Matthew had been remarkably tolerant of Jonathan's turbulent life. Matthew normally drove to the office and would be able to give Jonathan a lift, so he would not have to go by tube from Nicola's in Chiswick. On the tube, you could be jostled about and hurt your wrist further. And he had clothes in the wardrobe in Matthew's house.

I'll phone both Heather and Nicola tomorrow after the operation and put them off somehow, he thought, *I'll console Heather with the promise that when I have free days, she can collect me from Matthew's in her Ford Escort and drive me to our 'marital home'. I just hope she has not accepted any B&B guests during my next free days. I'll give her the dates on the phone tomorrow. But what shall I say to Nicola? She was badly disturbed having seen Carol kiss me. I'll explain about having to stay with Matthew and him driving me to work. Of course, Nicola will want to offer me a lift from her house to the office but luckily, she works in her teaching job in the mornings and driving me to work would make her late for hers. Yes, that's the solution, though she will be really disappointed. Oh, and I mustn't forget to phone Matthew, of course!*

Jonathan was right with his prediction that Nicola was deeply disappointed about not going to have him to stay. He could not dissuade her from wanting to visit him at Matt's in

Denham, and so she appeared there on several occasions a short while after Matt and Jonathan had got there after work. She had met Matt quite a few times before, and she found him agreeable as he either tended to watch TV in the living room while Jonathan and she went up to Jonathan's bedroom, or he would excuse himself and go to the pub for a drink. Denham had three pubs to choose from, and he alternated his watering holes, with his favourite being, *the Swan.*

The free days Jonathan had let Heather know about were approaching, and Nicola needed to know that there was no point in her driving to Denham then to see him there. What to do? Jonathan had already told her that he could not record matches elsewhere while his wrist was mending, so he could not use that as an excuse for his absence from Matt's house. During Nicola's last visit before Heather was due to collect him home, he had to bring Heather into play, much as it would hurt Nicola. They were lying in each other's arms in his bedroom at Matt's when Jonathan said, 'I'm afraid my ex-wife is in some sort of deep crisis which seems to be affecting her mental stability, and I'm really the only one she can turn to. She's coming to collect me by car the day after tomorrow, and I feel called upon to listen to her and try and soothe her. I'm only willing to do this as a helpful gesture from one human being to another, please understand, Nicola. I'll be off work for five days, and I'll ring you every day.'

Nicola did not say anything for a long while, fighting with tears. Then she said, 'You have to swear to me that there is nothing else going on, Jonathan! Why stay for five days when surely you can deal with her in just two!'

'Of course, I can swear nothing is going on! I'm afraid I'll be dependent on her driving me back to Denham, and she's bound to want me to stay for as long as possible.'

'It looks to me as though she is doing her utmost to have you back, and I don't like it, Jonathan! I think you're really weak, being at her beck and call.'

'I promise you, I don't want her back, Nicola. I've always thought you have a big, understanding heart. I'm just trying to help someone I've known for a long time.'

'Okay, you just go and play knight in shining armour but remember, I don't like it one little bit!'

And with that, they parted.

Jonathan felt awful lying again, and about something as serious as a non-existing mental breakdown and also annihilating the renewed, *marriage*, without a marriage certificate between him and Heather. If Heather knew!

He kept his promise to phone Nicola daily. To her mind, he pretended that he was having a hard time and that his patience was being tested because of Heather's erratic behaviour that he was counting the days until he could be with Nicola again. She was suspicious, and it unnerved her. She had been thinking that her relationship with Jonathan was leading nowhere, that she ought to be more cautious. However, she was also aware that she was obsessed with him and had already invested deep feelings in him, and the longer she was involved with him, the worse her obsession was likely to become.

20

When two close woman friends rang her from Belgium to suggest a walking tour in Britain together, Nicola felt that this would be just the right thing to do and offered to plan the route and book all the overnight accommodation. Her friends would be arriving in London in three weeks' time during Nicola's Easter holidays when she would not be doing any teaching of private courses for a change. They would spend the night before setting off at Nicola's house. They had agreed to Nicola's suggestion to walk a part of Offa's Dyke Path. Nicola decided not to tell Jonathan about her planned 7-day absence. Perhaps she could wean herself off him with the help of her good friends. Walking had always lent itself easily to talking, and her friends were sensible, grounded women.

Offa was the King of Mercia, and his path generally followed the English/Welsh border by way of 8th-century earthworks though in some places the Dyke had disappeared. The path covered open hill country, thick woods, pastoral lowlands and the floodplain of the River Severn. There would be outstanding scenery of natural beauty to marvel at, with medieval castles dotted along the way. They would need good walking boots, waterproof clothing, a map and a compass and walk with a rucksack on their backs. It would be too much to walk the entire length of the Path, 175 miles. Also, Nicola knew from having walked other long-distance paths that having to walk from accommodation to accommodation every single day soon took the holiday feeling out of the experience. She had therefore suggested, and her friends had agreed that after two days' walking, they should stay in the same place for two nights. That would give them a rest and the chance to stroll along the streets of a small town or village, have a leisurely cream tea in an old-fashioned tearoom, rummage in antique shops, and look at ancient churches and castles if they fancied. The three friends had agreed to start their walk at Chepstow and end it at Hay-on-Wye, a distance of 52 miles. They would use public transport to get to Chepstow and back to London from Hay. All they would need is dry weather! After the walk, and on their return to London Nicola would have to go back to teaching again but her friends would like to rent a car and stay in another area of England for some days, and they had asked Nicola to recommend a small town or village in the pretty countryside. When they next spoke to each other on the phone, Nicola gave her friends the phone number of a B&B in a village.

Thinking of their walk together, lovely thoughts sprang into Nicola's mind: away from the daily routine, away from the usual problems, with good friends, out in the countryside, getting pleasantly tired and fitter through exercise, being able to discuss the world's problems, and in particular one's own, having good and trusted listeners. What a pleasure! Nicola was looking forward to this break, hoping it would help her break away from Jonathan.

The next weeks were busy, with her booking the overnight accommodation along the path. She was preparing a list for

Zac and Ben with all the dates and places where they would be staying and the relevant phone numbers, just in case.

Helena, Susanna and Nicola had grown up together in the same neighbourhood of Leuven and gone to school together. Their parents were friends, and during their childhood summers, the three families would go on seaside holidays together on the Belgian coast, near Oostende. When the girls were in late teenage, they were allowed to travel across the border to either France or Germany during school holidays, staying in youth hostels. In Germany, they would explore the Romanesque churches and the cathedral in Cologne, the shrine of Charlemagne in Aix-la-Chapelle. In France, they would visit Reims, with its famous cathedral where numerous French kings had been crowned. In both places, they had certainly also visited cafes and beer gardens, museums and art galleries, and used their French and practised their German. Over the years, or rather decades, they had increasingly felt like sisters.

Both Susanna and Helena had made good careers, Susanna was running an interior design business, and Helena was working on a news channel on Belgian TV. They were both married, and each of them had two teenage children. Susanna had married Helena's brother Dirk, and so they were sisters-in-law.

21

Heather needed to book her car in for a service and took the booklet with the service record out of the glove compartment, ready to have this latest service entered. She turned the pages and there was the name and address of the previous owner. Nicola Hyatt. Nicola, Nicola? Jonathan had said this name on the phone when she had been listening on the other side of the door. A jolt went through Heather and her heart rate went up. Was there something going on between Jonathan and the woman he bought her car from? Unbelievable, it just could not be true. Perhaps there was another Nicola at the office in Acton, who needed to phone him.

A few days after Stella dropped in on her, the enormity of the choice Stella put to her was hitting Heather. She saddled her horse and went for a ride across the fields and through the woods. This was her customary way of doing her thinking. She was hunting her elusive thoughts, and the most important thing was to hunt down a decision. It went against the grain to have Jonathan observed and the findings reported to her. How she wished she could simply trust him! Also, she was petrified of getting a negative report as she would then have to act accordingly. There was a chance she might have again to go through what had so far been the darkest spell in her life.

On the other hand, if Jonathan had something to hide from her, she wanted to know in order to be in charge of her life. She also had to think about the cost which was likely to be considerable. But now that she did not have to pay back the bank loan any longer, she had plenty of money at her disposal, earned from her B&B business.

This was a decision which scared her. With great difficulty, she decided to consult a private investigator. On her return home, she looked up private investigators in the phone book and located one in Burford, just a few miles away. But she hesitated from week to week to contact someone in that office. The Easter holidays were drawing near, with her B&B fully booked because a lot of sports matches were taking place over Easter, and Jonathan would not be able to be at home. She would be too busy over Easter, so she forced herself to make that important phone call. She arranged a visit to the investigator's office. She had to bring a photo of Jonathan along, and the one she chose was one taken on their second honeymoon in the Dominican Republic.

She explained, 'I have to clarify to you that we have been divorced and technically still are, even though we've resumed our marriage with all the usual pledges, just without getting married to each other again. To my greatest disappointment, I've recently had suspicions that my so-to-speak husband has started another relationship with someone called Nicola. Here's her address.' And with that, she handed him a slip of paper. 'He bought a second-hand car from her for me.' She continued to fill him in on the past. The investigator, Sam, explained the fees. She pulled out her chequebook and made out a cheque to pay fees in advance. She was adamant that she never wanted to be sent a bill at her home address or be phoned at home. She would phone the office regularly, and if need be, send another cheque and go to the office to be briefed there. Because of the distance to London, she was told that the surveillance there would be subcontracted.

Heather phoned Stella to tell her of her decision.

'It must have been difficult to make up your mind, but this is good news, Heather,' said Stella, 'because you'll know one way or another instead of being burdened with suspicions. Well done! Any time you want to talk to me, I'll be there for you.'

'Thank you, Stella. It's good for me to know that.'

22

Jonathan's wrist had mended enough for him to drive again, the plaster had been removed, and he just needed to wear an elastic bandage for a while longer. Soon the old pattern was re-established. When he worked in or near London, he stayed with Nicola a couple of times a week and the rest with Matt in Denham, or Nicola went there and spent the odd night with Jonathan at Matt's house.

From time to time, he looked at Nicola wistfully and then said, 'I don't know what to do about you,' which did not fail to alarm Nicola.

He did not answer when she asked what that was supposed to mean but she knew it most likely had something to do with his ex-wife, ex, for Heaven's sake! She knew intuitively that there was something he withheld from her.

One evening when she was on her own, she got a big piece of paper out, spread it on the floor, knelt in front of it and drew a big triangle, above the corners she wrote the initials X and J and N. She tried to imagine what would happen to the stalemate if just one of these three changed something. If H dropped out, out of what? Well, out of the competition…suddenly, Nicola was clear about not wanting to marry Jonathan ever. He was unreliable, not trustworthy. If she dropped out, he would continue with Heather but cheat on her with other women. It was as simple as that. There was now the hope that her head might rule her heart, after all.

But when she thought of Jonathan, she still longed for his presence. How would she ever have the strength to do without him? Still, she stuck to her decision not to tell him of her planned Offa's Dyke walk with her childhood friends. It would be interesting to find out how he would react.

23

During the last week before the Easter break, an ESL team meeting had been called by the team leader, Richard. They went back to basics by defining what ESL stood for: English as a Second Language.

Rose stated, 'The objective cannot be bilingualism for these adult immigrants.'

Nicola agreed, 'To be realistic, it would be a more reachable goal to leave it at English becoming a secondary language for them in which they could somehow function, and, I hope, function enough to find work eventually.'

They listed the reasons for Richard, though he should have been keenly aware of the difficulties of their teaching situation from one or two visits he had paid when their classes were in progress, and Rose said:

'Look, Richard, the students' ages range from teenage to their seventies, and they come from many different countries, India, Pakistan, Sri Lanka, Afghanistan, Chile and even Bulgaria and Poland.'

Nicola interrupted, 'Yes, a relatively high number of these countries are war zones, and many students have been traumatised.'

Rose continued, 'And now, most of our students experience culture shock, and here they share a classroom with people their countries have been or still are at war with.'

Nicola voiced another thought, 'Having to learn to write in another script just seems a minor extra problem, and, Richard, do you realise that outside the classroom there's very little need for our students to use English?'

Rose explained in detail, 'They don't use it with their families and neighbours, and not when shopping, going to a dentist's, doctor's, travel agency, solicitor's, driving school and many more places.'

They could use their mother tongue, be it Gujarati, Punjabi, Hindi, Urdu, Arabic, Farsi or Tamil.

Richard admitted, 'I didn't fully realise what you're up against and I'm surprised and see that it will take so much longer for the students to be able to operate in English. But on another note, I've found another classroom in Wellspring School which I'd like Nicola to use after the Easter holidays, okay, Nicola?'

'That will be very helpful, thanks, Richard,' she answered.

She felt very glad, especially as she would have her very own board there. Her two colleagues would then not face any more negotiations about the board in the Council Chamber, one could use the board before, the other after the break.

The meeting concluded, and on the way back home, Nicola stopped at the nearby school to inspect the new classroom. It was in an old prefab in the playground of the school. There was indeed a board to write on, but Nicola noticed a puddle on the floor of the classroom and remembered yesterday's rain. It meant that the roof was leaking and was also a hazard in case anyone slipped on a wet floor and got hurt. She went in search of the school caretaker and asked for a bucket and a mop to be placed permanently in this classroom. Once home, she phoned Richard.

'Richard, Nicola here. I stopped at the school on my way home to look at the classroom. Have you seen it? No? Well, it's in an old prefab.'

She reported the unsuitability of this classroom to him and the ensuing problems with Health and Safety regulations.

She urged him, 'Please, can you secure another, safer classroom I can use after the Easter break?'

Helena and Susanna arrived at Heathrow and were on their way to Nicola's house. She had been busy on this last day of teaching before the Easter holidays. On her return from teaching at lunchtime, she had started preparing a delicious evening meal for the five of them, including Zac and Ben. This was not the first time Susanna and Helena had visited her in Chiswick. The big oak table was laid in Nicola's cosy kitchen.

Nicola had pinned an itinerary on the noticeboard in the kitchen with the dates, addresses and phone numbers of all the places they would be staying at during the walk. Nicola did not have a mobile phone, so to check on Zac and Ben she would have to call from a phone box. Among these places where they would be staying were B&Bs, youth hostels and one or two hotels in town centres. Where possible, Nicola had booked triple rooms, a special request by her friends to relive their teenage this way, talking in the dark. She repeated to Zac and Ben that they should not divulge her whereabouts to Jonathan, should he phone or come by the house.

Nicola had also already bought their railway tickets from Paddington to Chepstow for the following morning. It would be a mid-morning start, but the train journey would only take two and a half hours, so they would have lunch in Chepstow and have time to visit the castle there, having left their rucksacks at their accommodation. Nicola had also pre-booked the hire car her friends would be using for a few days after their return to London to stay in a B&B in another pretty part of England they wanted to explore.

The doorbell was ringing, it was her friends! After a noisy welcome, she showed them to their bedroom, and they had afternoon tea together. Both Helena and Susanna were amazed at how grown-up Zac and Ben were. They had not seen each other for a couple of years. The boys liked their mum's friends. They were like extended family. They had been on a number of visits, often without their mum, to both Susanna and Helena and their families in Leuven. They all spoke Flemish to each other and had a jolly evening together with plenty of wine.

In the course of the evening, Nicola asked Helena and Susanna, 'By the way, have you booked your stay in the B&B I recommended to you on the phone?'

Susanna answered, 'Yes, we did that straightaway.'

Their confirmation of that sent a quick shiver down Nicola's spine. The boys excused themselves and went to their rooms to listen to music or watch TV.

Susanna talked about her design business and described a flat she had recently been asked to furnish in art deco style.

'It was so much fun despite being quite a challenge. I designed a wallpaper for the living room and a different one for the bedrooms in the flat. The owners also wanted a carpet in art deco style, which I designed myself because I couldn't find one second-hand. I commissioned this carpet to be woven and the wallpaper to be printed. I found art deco wall lamps and vases in various antique shops. The finished flat looks stunning if I may say so myself. And do you know what? A design magazine has asked to take photos to go with an article for the June issue, and my contact details will be printed at the end of the article. That will be so good for my business!'

'That is fantastic, Susanna!' cried Nicola. 'Please get an extra copy of that magazine for me in June. How is work for you, Helena?'

'I'm now working on the evening TV news and often have to go out and interview people like politicians and scientists during the day. So, I really have to do my homework beforehand! I meet really interesting and important people many of whom have a big ego, and as you know, politicians are skilled in never answering the questions you put to them. Work can be quite stressful, but I love the challenge. It sometimes gives me the feeling of achieving something against the odds. How about you, Nicola?'

'I'd love to be sure that I'm achieving something with my teaching, I must say! My goal is to prepare my students to apply for jobs and get into employment. The problem is my students all live in a suburb where they can get by without a word of English. Students from other European countries who come here for a year as au pairs have a much better chance of getting closer to being bilingual when taking courses in English as a Foreign Language for one of the Cambridge exams. And why? It's because at school they've learnt how to learn. So, one of the most important components of my lessons is to teach learning strategies.'

'Your job sounds incredibly complex, with so many hurdles, Nicola,' Susanna and Helena agreed.

'Yes, you can say that again! There's so much more which is really trying about my job, but this is your first night here, so let's raise our glasses, cheers!'

They chatted on, Nicola replenished their glasses and finally asked if her friends would like a cup of coffee.

'Thank you,' Susanna said, 'but I think I'll head for bed, because we'll have an early start tomorrow.' And Helena joined her.

24

The private investigator had sent a subcontracted London-based private eye, Tom, to the Acton office where Jonathan worked, and he had followed Jonathan's car back to Denham. Of course, Heather had been able to give Sam Matt's address in Denham. Following the car was made easy by the highly noticeable colour of Jonathan's car. Not once had Tom lost sight of the bright orange Mercedes, even on the M-40. Tom had to be careful not to come to Jonathan's attention in Denham where there was hardly a person to be seen on foot. That is why he parked his grey car at some distance and sat on a bench on the village green with a newspaper, with Matt's house in view where Jonathan had disappeared into. Thank goodness it was not raining as half an hour passed before there was more action. Another car drew up in front of Matt's house, and a man climbed out with luggage and unlocked the door to the house, like Jonathan. This would be his friend, Matt. Another thirty minutes later, both men left the house on foot and make for, *the Swan*. Tom decided to try and get some idea of what their conversation was about by standing quite close to them but with his back turned at the bar. They asked for pints of London Pride, 'Two pints of London Pride, please, and a couple of bags of crisps, salt and vinegar.'

Tom also ordered a pint for himself. They sat down near the door to the pub garden, and Tom stayed within earshot.

'That week's work in Edinburgh has been tough, and I've been pining for a London Pride. How is Heather these days?' asked Matt.

'Oh, she's fine. Her B&B is going well. She's fully booked over the Easter period because I'll have to work. You know, I'm not keen on stumbling over all these guests when I come to stay, so I always let her know when she can accept guests.'

'And how is Nicola?'

'Ah, she's still gorgeous and exciting but just recently she's been a bit cagey. I have the notion that she's cooling our relationship a bit and is always on about what I told her, namely that Heather is my ex-wife, with her emphasis on "ex." She sees no point whatsoever to continue seeing an ex-partner after a divorce, just because she never wants to see her ex.'

Tom had Nicola's address from the service record of Heather's car and had already been outside Nicola's house and watched it from a café opposite. He had only seen two boys in their late teenage go in and leave, no woman who could be their mother.

There was just this overheard conversation in the pub to report, which Tom phoned through to Sam in Burford. When Heather phoned Sam a couple of days later, she was upset to hear the name, *Nicola*, mentioned which confirmed her worst fears. But she was still full of self-recriminations and shame as to spying on Jonathan. She had no idea what she was going to do with this information. She could not imagine confronting Jonathan with what she had been told because she was ashamed of using a private investigator. However, she told Sam that she wanted the surveillance to continue for the time being.

25

The three women friends arrived in Chepstow and spent the afternoon sightseeing. The castle was the oldest post-Roman structure in Britain and overlooked the river Wye, which they would be more or less following on either bank on the walk to Hay-on-Wye as it formed the border between England and Wales for part of the way. The castle and its setting above the river appealed to Helena and Susanna's idea of Romanticism and they had both taken a number of photos of it. The weather was dry and forecast to stay so for the next couple of days. Tomorrow's walk was to break them in gently, just 8 miles. But the rucksacks seemed so heavy! They unpacked everything at the B&B where they were staying the first night.

'Oh, Susanna and Nicola.' Helena giggled. 'We've each of us taken along such large bottles of shampoo and big tubes of toothpaste!'

'Let's just take one of each with us and leave the rest in the bathroom for future guests or our hosts to use. That will make a difference to the weight we'll have to carry,' suggested Helena.

They had a pleasant pub meal in the evening and the three friends decided on an early night. The next night's accommodation was a B&B near Tintern Abbey, set in meadows in a Welsh valley. The Abbey would certainly appeal even more to Susanna and Helena's sense of Romanticism. It was built in the 13th Century and still was remarkably whole, with its transept arches standing 70 feet high, and the seven lights of the west window undamaged in any detail. William Wordsworth, England's most renowned Romantic poet, even wrote a poem, *Lines written a few miles above Tintern Abbey*.

'How's your love life?' Susanna and Helena asked Nicola during the walk, and Nicola launched into the long story of how she met Jonathan, her hunch that he was still attached to his ex-wife and that he was not really free, about her seeing Carol at the hospital.

She admitted, 'I'm afraid I'm still hooked on him but also have second thoughts that the relationship isn't good for me. I feel anxious most of the time, even suspicious. I haven't told Jonathan of our walk and asked the boys not to tell him how to reach me in case he phones or comes by the house.'

'That makes a lot of sense, Nicola,' commented her friends.

'I must confess, I see our days away together as my chance to distance myself from him with your moral support,' added Nicola.

It was so good to walk with close friends through beautiful valleys with a river view, through woods and fields, and to feel understood.

She plucked up courage and told them, 'I have a role for you to play, in other words, the B&B I recommended to you in the Cotswold is run by Heather, Jonathan's ex-wife. Do you mind?'

Both Susanna and Helena screamed with delight at playing private detectives for Nicola. That sounded like a thrilling adventure. They agreed that Nicola's relationship with Jonathan sounded too complex, that he was likely to be playing a devious game and that she was clearly suffering whereas a relationship should make her happy, as she deserved in their opinion.

Nicola had phoned the English Tourist Board and asked if there was a B&B in Milton-under-Wychwood which had once been a smithy.

'Oh, you must mean the B&B which calls itself "The Old Smithy" then,' she was told.

'Could you give me the owner's name and phone number, please?'

This is how Nicola found out that the ex-wife was called Heather.

26

Heather had a booking by phone for five days during the Easter period from an interesting-sounding man from Bristol. He booked a single room which could be given to three people, so Heather did not mind sleeping on the sofa in the office, to make full use of the demand for rooms during the Easter break. What made him interesting to her, quite apart from his pleasant voice, was that he enquired if he could hire her horse during this time.

'Do you ride regularly, then? I mean, do you know how to handle a horse? The paths around Milton-under-Wychwood can be walked, a horse is not strictly necessary to explore the countryside round here.'

'Yes, I'm used to riding horses. I started as a child and have kept riding all my life. I'm a vet and live on the outskirts of Bristol. I would like to publish a book on footpaths, rights of ways and bridleways in West Oxfordshire, accompanied by photos, and nothing seems to have been published about the area around Milton-under-Wychwood. I will need to explore in all directions, and it just would take too long on foot. So, when I saw on your website that you hire out your horse to riders, I knew yours is the B&B I want to stay in.'

'That's wonderful. What name can I put and when can I expect you on your arrival day?'

'The name is George Hunter, and I think I should be arriving at about 4 pm on that Tuesday. I would like to take dinner in the evenings at your B&B as well. It would be ever so helpful if I could book a packed lunch each day because I will probably find myself in the middle of nowhere at lunchtime during my rides out. Just put those packed lunches with everything else on my bill, please. So, see you on Tuesday afternoon! Bye.'

'A good trip here!'

Heather found herself thinking about George Hunter from time to time. She was curious to meet him early next week. He was the first guest to want to hire her horse for more than an hour's ride, five entire days even! She liked the fact that he was a vet. He was bound to treat Dinah well. Her income from him would be considerable as he had not just booked bed and breakfast but the packed lunches, dinner and her horse as well. She hoped he would like his stay and want to return. It would take him more than five days to explore all the footpaths and bridle paths around Milton-under-Wychwood, surely!

27

Jonathan had phoned Nicola's number a couple of times, in vain. He was puzzled. She was usually at home in the afternoons. Perhaps she was out shopping. On his third try, the phone was picked up by Zac.

'Hello, Zac, Jonathan here. How are things with you?'

'Fine, and you?'

'Well. You know, busy. Can I speak to your mum?'

'She's out at the moment.'

'Do you know when she will be back?'

'No, she must have left before I got home from college.'

'Fine, I'll try again! Bye.'

Later the same day, Jonathan made repeat phone calls, without success. Therefore, he decided to come by Nicola's house in the early evening. Her car was in the drive, a good sign. He rang the doorbell and had to wait for a few minutes before the door was answered by Ben.

'Hi, there, Ben! How are things?'

'Fine, Jonathan, come in and have a beer.'

'I don't mind if I do, thanks.'

On entering the kitchen, Jonathan noticed the list pinned on the notice board, in Nicola's handwriting. He studied it in amazement, and pointing at the board, asked Ben, 'What is all this about?'

Ben was trapped and had to give an explanation.

'Mum's friends from Belgium came and they have gone off on a walk, and these here are the dates and places where they will be staying.'

'She didn't even mention this to me,' Jonathan sounded most offended.

'Well, they might have decided on this on the spur of the moment,' Ben said in futile consolation.

When Jonathan had left, Ben thought he should phone his mum to let her know that Jonathan had seen the list. But he was off to a party that night and forgot.

Jonathan was in a frenzy. What was this supposed to mean? He was hurt and also in a rage. This was not the Nicola he knew. She always planned in advance, there was no way that she had left on the spur of the moment, least of all with two friends who had arrived from Belgium. It was a purposeful affront to him and was all arranged weeks ago, he was sure. He felt so frustrated as he was fully booked for work.

The three women had left Tintern after a good breakfast and were well on their way to Monmouth, their next overnight stop, and as agreed, after two days' walking, they would be staying in the same spot for two nights. They were looking forward to being in Monmouth, which their guidebook had described as the finest town on Offa's Dyke Walk. It was a beautiful market town, busy and urbane, with a unique fortified bridge and a castle of which just the keep was still left standing. Next to it was the Great Castle House from the 17th century, made of red sandstone, a local building material.

It had a noble design, according to the Renaissance ideas of perfection, quite alien to South Wales. Henry V was born here, as well as Mr Rolls of Rolls-Royce fame, of whom there was even a statue in Agincourt Square, the main square. There would be plenty to do and see as there was also a Local History Museum. They were especially looking forward to staying in the main hotel, *the King's Arms*, which had its own restaurant and bar.

Today's walk was longer than yesterday's, and they walked through woods alternating with open hill country. They had bought sandwiches and bottles of water before setting off from Tintern to have a picnic at lunchtime. They sat on flat rocks for lunch and enjoyed a wide view of the countryside.

'Isn't this wonderful? Look at that view! We're so lucky.' And with that Helena handed the sandwiches around.

'I'm just thinking that my students will hardly ever have got out into the English countryside and have been stuck in London most of the time,' Nicola mused.

In mid-afternoon, they had finally reached the outskirts of Monmouth and were walking in single file along the main road for the last two miles into town when Nicola suddenly thought she had seen an orange car whizz by. She was alarmed but both Susanna and Helena calmed her down.

'It would just be too much of a coincidence, Nicola, and other people also have orange cars, even if that is pretty rare. You said Jonathan has to work, anyway, and also, Zac and Ben are under orders not to speak to Jonathan about this trip, so, don't worry! Did you see the make of the car, by the way?'

'No, I didn't, I only saw an orange flash go by.'

They had reached Agincourt Square and were admiring the front of the ancient building with a coat of arms above the main entrance to *the King's Arms*. Nicola had seen a sign, *Hotel Car Park*, and slowly walked around the corner of the hotel and, to her consternation, she spotted Jonathan's orange Mercedes in the hotel car park. This was a bombshell. She whispered to Helena and Susanna who felt her alarm. Nicola made sure she was the last of the three to enter the hotel. She peered over their shoulders. From the check-in desk, you could see into the bar where a smiling Jonathan was sitting, observing them. By the time the formalities were over, Jonathan was standing beside the three friends and leant towards Nicola with the words, 'Fancy seeing you here!'

'That's just what I wanted to say,' Nicola snapped back, 'what on earth do you think you're doing here?'

'I was only longing to see you, Nicola darling,' replied Jonathan, 'and perhaps you'll introduce me to your friends.'

Nicola reluctantly made the introductions, and Jonathan conjured up all his charm. He invited the three women for drinks in the bar and dinner in the hotel restaurant afterwards. Helena and Susanna accepted with pleasure and turned to the staircase to go up to their triple room, and before Nicola could follow them, Jonathan had held Nicola back.

'Why are you here? Who gave you this address?' Nicola hissed.

'Why didn't you tell me of this trip, Nicola? I phoned your number several times and then went to the house. Only Ben was in, and he let me into the kitchen where I saw the list which explained everything, and I memorised where you'd be staying tonight. It was really difficult to find someone to stand in for me at work for a couple of days. But here I am.'

'You have no business to be here. I'm having a lovely break with my childhood friends, that's why I didn't mention this trip to you.'

'Calm down, Nicola, let's have a nice time while we can! I booked a double ensuite for you and me here.'

'My friends and I have booked a triple room, and for the entire walk I will be sharing a room with my two friends.'

Jonathan thought he could persuade Nicola later to change her mind, after a few glasses of pre-dinner drinks and wine, so he was quite relaxed about her answer.

Nicola joined her friends in their bedroom, and after a shower and good rest, the three of them changed into the only slightly more elegant outfits they had brought along in their rucksacks, smarter trousers and pretty, silky tops, all a bit creased.

She asked them, 'Can you imagine what Jonathan said to me downstairs? He'd gone ahead and booked a double room for himself and me, but I swear I won't forsake you in our room tonight just to satisfy a whim of Jonathan's.'

Susanna and Helena noticed how shaken Nicola was.

The bar was as cosy as a womb, with a thick carpet in muted colours, and a huge fireplace which had a crackling wood fire going in it. April in Wales could be chilly, especially in the evenings, and looking at the flames was mesmerising. The walls were covered in green and gold striped wallpaper and sported brass lamps which cast a warm light. They found a corner bench and a table near the fireplace.

Jonathan was his usual talkative self while they were having drinks in the bar, telling jokes and getting the laughs he craved, a put-on show for the three. The dinner he had invited them for was splendid, they had chosen a starter of various dips, traditional roasts, trimmed with a selection of vegetables, followed by delicious mousse au Chocolat. All that was rinsed down with plenty of expensive Mouton de Rothschild. Later, in the bar for nightcaps, Susanna and Helena were sitting a little apart from Nicola and Jonathan to let them talk.

Nicola hissed at Jonathan, 'I've made a decision, Jonathan. You've got exactly one month to decide between me and your ex-wife.'

He was really taken aback and seemed confused. 'You surely can't mean that, Nicola?' The last thing he expected from Nicola was an ultimatum.

She repeated, 'She's your ex, ex, ex, remember? In exactly one month from now, I expect a definite answer, it's either her or me. The date is in my diary. Also, we might or might not see you at breakfast. We'll have a late one because we are staying here a second night, and you will probably have to have an early start so you can work again the day after tomorrow. Good night, Jonathan.'

And with that, the three got up, thanked him for drinks and dinner and went up to their room.

'Did you notice, Susanna,' Helena said, 'he wasn't wearing a wedding ring.'

'Yes, I noticed that, too!'

'Here in the UK many married men don't always wear a wedding ring, so that doesn't have to mean anything,' commented Nicola.

'Tell me, what did you think of him?'

'What can I say, Nicola, he isn't the most stunning-looking man, but he certainly has a lot of charm to make up for it and seems to feel at ease in female company. It was nice of him to invite us for drinks and dinner.'

'Don't forget he had an ulterior motive, girls! I told you earlier this afternoon that he has booked a double room for himself and me, and I'm really proud I had the strength to decline it a second time after dinner in the bar when he urged me again and started whispering sweet nothings.'

'Yes, well done, Nicola, that will give him food for thought!'

'You don't know the best part yet! I've given him an ultimatum between Heather and myself, and he has to give me his decision in exactly a month's time.'

They talked for a long time in the dark as they did as teenagers and analysed everything that had been said since their arrival at the hotel.

28

It was Tuesday afternoon, and a Land Rover drew up in front of, *The Old Smithy*. Heather watched a slim man in his mid-40s get out of the car. George Hunter had a shock of unruly black hair, dark eyes and a healthy complexion. He fetched his travel bag and used the door knocker rather than the bell. Heather answered the door and greeted him,

'Mr Hunter? Welcome! How was your trip here?'

'Good afternoon, Mrs Shilling, it went really smoothly, thank you.'

She showed him to his room upstairs. He seemed impressed by the house so far and smiled appreciatively.

Heather asked him, 'Can I offer you a cup of tea or coffee downstairs in the kitchen/dining room?'

And he settled for a cup of tea. His voice was soft and gentle, and he came across as really warm and friendly.

He asked her, 'Can you tell me something about the history of the house? That would interest me.'

Heather liked talking about it. 'Yes, certainly. It used to be the smithy when the village street was built in the late 18th century. In fact, the old anvil is still here, if you want to see it.'

'Definitely, and could I also see your horse?'

Heather led him out of the back door into the garden, where the daffodils were out in force. She showed him the old anvil in an outhouse and then Dinah in her stable. Heather noticed immediately that he knew how to handle a horse by the way he approached and talked to it in a sensitive way. He patted Dinah, and it was clear from her reaction that she was at ease with him. He asked a number of questions about the horse and stroked her muzzle while listening to Heather's answers.

They returned to the kitchen and had another cup of tea while Heather asked what sort of things he would like as sandwich fillings for his lunches. He was modest, not fussy at all. He talked about his footpath mission with a passion and mentioned William Cobbett's book, *Rural Rides*, which had inspired him.

She gave him the time when dinner would be ready, and he set off on foot to explore the village for a while. There were six other guests around the dinner table, from Canada, New Zealand and England, apart from George and Heather, and the conversation was animated and flowed easily. It turned out to be a really enjoyable evening. All her dinner guests complimented her on the meal. Heather felt very taken by George Hunter's manner, so when he returned from an evening walk after dinner, she caught him in the hallway and offered him a nightcap, which he gladly accepted.

She asked him, 'What sort of animals do you deal with as a vet?'

She was pleased to learn that he did not look after budgerigars, hamsters and cats but located as he was on the outskirts of Bristol, his clients were farmers and he tended to farm animals and horses. He noticed that the fireplace in the living room where they were sitting had no wood piled up next to it.

He offered, 'Tomorrow morning, I'll chop some logs up before I set off for the day.'

It was indeed chilly in the room, and Heather explained, 'My husband's working away from home at the moment, and I've run out of wood to burn but there are huge logs by the garden shed. How very nice of you to offer your help!'

She was interested enough to look at his left hand to see if he was wearing a wedding ring. He was not but then she knew it could still mean that he was married. Not every husband was wearing a ring like Jonathan.

29

After a pleasant day pottering around and a second night in Monmouth, the three women friends continued on their walk. Soon after leaving Monmouth, they had a choice of paths, the Castle Route or the main one, and the three opted for, the *Castle Path*, following the river Monnow.

Nicola explained, 'Imagine this! I've been invited to the Hindu wedding of one of my female students from India towards the end of the summer term!'

Her friends found that exciting. 'Such a dip into a different culture will be an exciting experience. You'll have to describe it to us afterwards, Nicola!'

It was drizzling steadily and before they decided to get their raingear out of their rucksacks, they were pretty drenched and needed to change their t-shirts. So, for a few minutes, three women were standing in a clearing taking off their t-shirts and bras and rummaging around for dry ones out of their luggage. The castles appeared in a fine mist, which made them look even more romantic, like in Chinese or Japanese paintings. Susanna, Helena and Nicola never ran out of conversation. They talked about their jobs, their children, and planned holidays, Helena and Susanna talked about their husbands and Nicola only sometimes about Jonathan, anything she had previously forgotten to mention.

'I can't help speculating what Heather and her B&B might be like,' Helena said.

Susanna agreed, 'I wonder what sort of person she is.'

Nicola added, 'I know Heather is a couple of years older than Jonathan, so she'd have to be about 43 years old now, I reckon. I also have a hunch that the house is quite spectacular, a real country residence. Jonathan has gone on and on about it. Oh, you must take a lot of photos of it and its interior, maybe you can even of Heather.'

They enjoyed the rhythm of two days walking, and then staying in the same place for a couple of nights. They loved cosy evenings eating hearty meals in ancient pubs. They felt as close to each other as they did as teenagers. Their last two nights were spent in Hay-on-Wye. Susanna and Helena were amazed at the number of bookshops in this small town.

Nicola told them, 'A lot of the literary festivals take place here, with famous authors reading from their works.'

The three spent hours browsing in the bookshops, no wonder their rucksacks became heavier for the trip back.

The way back to London on Sunday took a long time because it was more convoluted. They first needed to catch a bus to Hereford, go from there to Newport by train and change trains there for Paddington. On their arrival at Nicola's house, both Zac and Ben greeted the three. As a surprise, they had concocted a meal, a big salad and macaroni cheese. There were several bottles of red wine, too.

Nicola felt really proud of them. 'Boys, that's such a lovely welcome from you! Imagine, Jonathan turned up, completely out of the blue.'

A blushing Ben said, 'Mum, I'm really sorry. He came by the house and entered the kitchen, then studied the list of dates and addresses, and I didn't think he'd memorise them.'

Nicola assured him, 'Don't worry, Ben, we coped okay with him in Monmouth.'

Nicola would not have time for lesson planning for Monday, so would have to improvise the next day at work, but she was an experienced teacher with plenty of ideas up her sleeve. Her friends would be picking up the rental car nearby and setting off for Milton-under-Wychwood. They were a bit apprehensive about driving on the left, but Nicola assured them.

'Just remember that drivers in the roundabout have priority. No need to worry! I can't wait for your return on Friday with lots of interesting things for you to report! See you in four days!'

As could be predicted, Jonathan phoned that afternoon. 'Nicola, my darling, it's me! I simply must see you tonight.'

Nicola was in a better mood, having had a successful teaching session in the morning, even without preparation, and a promising meeting with her team leader, Richard, after class.

'Well, Jonathan, would you like to come around to my house at 7:30?'

'Ah, that sounds wonderful! Till later, Nicola!'

Tom followed him there in his grey car and saw Jonathan entering Nicola's house. He decided to be in the café opposite very early in the morning to check if Jonathan left Nicola's house then, camera at the ready.

Nicola missed the backup from her friends and ended up being far mellower than she was in Monmouth. Part of her was still longing to be with Jonathan, despite all she had said. Could one call it a relapse? Perhaps. They shared what was left of the macaroni cheese, and Jonathan had contributed a bottle of wine. After dinner, they collapsed on the sofa in the living room, listened to music and started stroking and kissing each other.

Jonathan asked, 'You can't have meant that about the ultimatum, Nicola, that was a bad joke, surely!'

'Oh, no, it wasn't, Jonathan. I'm deadly serious about this. I can't go on living in uncertainty. You have to make a clear decision, and time is already ticking away. You have roughly three weeks left.'

'I felt really rejected when you wouldn't share the double room with me at the hotel. It hurt!'

'My friends and I had agreed that we would share triple rooms on this trip, and your surprise appearance was no reason to change that, Jonathan!'

To change the topic, Jonathan asked, 'Have your friends left?'

And Nicola answered, 'Yes.'

Ha, she thought, *this is not a lie, they've left my house.*

'You've got really nice friends, I liked them,' he continued.

'Yes, I've known them since childhood and all our parents have been friends for decades. We're like sisters, all the same age, we went to school together, and Susanna and Helena actually ended up as sisters-in-law.'

'That's really unusual, how astonishing!'

The orange Mercedes stayed parked outside Nicola's house as Tom noted when he checked again shortly after midnight on his way home from another mission. It was still there at 6 in the morning. Luckily, the Café opposite opened really early, and Tom took a window seat. He was on his third cup of latte when the door to Nicola's house opened at 8:15 am and Jonathan came out. Tom took a furtive photo of Jonathan, which did not go unnoticed by the Café owner. Tom scribbled the date, time and place down on his notepad. The photo would also clearly show Nicola's house number as well as the orange Mercedes parked in front of her house. His report, together with the enlarged photo would reach Sam in Burford in a couple of days. It was a busy week for Tom because the next late afternoon he followed Nicola's car. He had seen it parked in her driveway a few times and had noted down the registration number, and it soon became evident that she was heading in the direction of Denham.

In Denham, Nicola and Jonathan headed for *the Swan* for a meal, and Tom succeeded in snapping a photo of them together. Nicola's car was still parked outside Matt's house in the small hours. Sam would see in Thursday's post that Tom had been busy!

30

Before Nicola left for the first teaching session after the Easter break on Monday, she phoned Richard, the team leader.

'Richard here, good morning!'

'Richard, it's Nicola here. Can I see you after my teaching session this morning, please?'

'Let me see…when can you make it here to the office?'

'About 12:30.'

'Yes, that will be okay.'

'Ah, one more thing, Richard. Have you been able to secure another classroom for me without a leaking roof?'

'Sorry, but I'm still trying to find a better alternative.'

'That's a real pity, Richard. Next time it rains, the Health and Safety regulations will be broken.'

'It's on my mind. See you later, Nicola.'

Nicola drove to Richard's office after the lessons. Richard welcomed her, and she reminded him that in the last meeting, all three teachers had agreed that the main purpose of the lessons had to be launching their adult students into employment.

She continued, 'I'd like to make a linguistic analysis of the necessary language to work in a factory canteen, and then, I can pre-teach this in class. This kind of work, like washing up and preparing vegetables, won't require years of training even for those with just rudimentary English. And those of my students who are more advanced and confident might like to serve food to the workers when they have their breaks. We could practise this in class by doing role-play.'

Richard was listening with interest and nodded encouragingly.

'Could I have a week off during this summer term so I can spend it in a factory canteen to make my analysis, and then prepare the relevant teaching materials?'

Richard made to get up, but Nicola had not finished yet.

'One of my oldest students is from India. He retired after working in British factories for 40 years. You know, he had come to England shortly after Partition when factory workers were so urgently needed after the war. He's finally had the time to attend English classes. He speaks English fluently, can read and write, but his English is "fossilised", grammatically incorrect. He's such an asset in my class. He translates when necessary and listens to individual students read. He told me that by law one worker on each factory floor must have a First Aid certificate. Having one would mean an increased chance of employment. Could you let me invite a Red Cross First Aid instructor into the classroom to teach my students? I think all my students have a chance of passing the test, and for many, the certificate would possibly be the first-ever achievement in their lives. This would boost their self-confidence and motivation.'

'Oh, Nicola, these are good ideas. I'll contact one of the factories along the A4 towards Heathrow to ask for a placement for you,' Richard promised.

'I'm really thrilled, Richard, and will contact the local Red Cross office to find out if one of the officers there would be free to teach First Aid to my class.'

She would like to put both her ideas into practice during this summer term. It would be a very busy one!

31

Susanna and Helena enjoyed their drive on Monday, once they had left London and its traffic behind. They chose a route through villages rather than staying on the motorway where possible and finally arrived in Milton-under-Wychwood. Getting out of the car in front of the B&B, located on the wide main road through the village, they were excited to see a thatched roof on the whitewashed house with smallish windows, like in the pictures on the chocolate boxes you could buy in England. Helena had already taken a photo of it when the front door opened, and a kind-looking woman stepped out and introduced herself as Heather Shilling. She had wavy medium-length hair which was slightly greying, a round, friendly face and blue eyes. She was wearing trousers and a sweater. There was nothing pretentious about her.

She greeted them, 'Welcome! You must be Susanna and Helena! Come on in!'

They followed her along the hall, hung with pictures of hunting scenes, and up the thickly carpeted stairs to their bedroom. On the outside of the door was a framed picture of a William Morris wallpaper design, inscribed with the words, *Strawberry Thief.*

'Yes, you are in "Strawberry Thief",' Heather pointed out.

They turned their heads, and indeed, the other bedroom doors showed similar signs, two of Morris' wallpaper called, *Seaweed* and *Pimpernel*, and a non-Morris one, *Poppies and Cornflowers.*

Oh, my God, thought Susanna, the interior design expert, *what will await us inside our room?*

They had booked a twin room, and this room contained a double and a single bed which seem to be surrounded by a garden full of birds and strawberries. Apart from the *Strawberry Thief* wallpaper, the curtains and bedspreads showed the same pattern. It was all a bit overwhelming, especially for someone who favoured the stark Bauhaus style. The room, however, was as cosy as a nest, and it overlooked the front of the house. Heather showed them their ensuite bathroom, the TV and remote control, and the tea/coffee-making facilities, such a standard in English B&Bs. She invited them for a cup of tea or coffee downstairs in the dining room/kitchen, and they gladly accepted. Once Heather had left them, they threw themselves onto the beds, laughing and giggling.

'Oh, this will be a fascinating stay, Susanna!'

'I'm going to take photos of this room before we go downstairs, Helena! I can't believe that anyone would smother a room in plant and bird motifs like that! How twee, naming rooms after wallpaper designs!'

Downstairs, they chose a cup of coffee, being from the Continent, called *Europe* by plenty of British people. The L-shaped kitchen/dining room was spacious. The oak kitchen cupboards looked fine with the soft glow of brown wood, and around the corner was a huge oak dining table where Heather served the coffee and sat down with them.

'Where are you from?' she asked.

'We're from Belgium.'

'Have you travelled from there today?'

'No, we stayed with a friend in London overnight. Can you tell us yet what time dinner is tonight, and have you got other guests staying?'

Of course, they had booked dinner every night, in order to observe Heather as much as possible, and for convenience's sake. After touring around the area all day, and having lunch in a pub, they cherished the thought of not having to go out for dinner as well.

'Dinner is at 7:30, and I just have another couple of guests staying right now.'

'We look forward to meeting them tonight, then. Did the village smith live in this house in the old days?'

Heather delighted in telling them about the history of the house and also mentioned the anvil and her horse. Of course, they asked if they could see both, and Heather led them towards the back door. On the way out, they noticed a big horse calendar on the kitchen wall by the back door. They were enthusiastic about the old anvil and, of course, took a photo of it and the outbuilding where it was housed. They loved the horse and asked her name, stroked and patted her, and Heather told them about her frequent rides through the surrounding countryside, and how much she loved it. They decided to go for a stroll through the village but not until they had taken a photo of Heather standing by Dinah.

'Thanks for the coffee and see you at dinner, Heather!'

'Have you noticed, Helena, that Heather is wearing a wedding ring?'

'Yes, I have, and to be honest, I'm quite astonished. I simply didn't expect that of a divorced woman, unless she is in fact still married to him! What does it mean in relation to Jonathan? His not wearing one could still mean that he is married to Heather. As Nicola explained, a man not wearing a wedding ring can mean both that he's married and not married.'

'Let me get this straight, Susanna, what if he lied to Nicola that he was buying her car for his "ex"-wife?'

'Yes, he might well have lied to her to persuade her that he was free to enter into a relationship. Something is fishy here. I can feel it. It was her husband she phoned when the tap was dripping, I'm sure. Do you remember what Nicola told us about him lying to Heather on the phone?'

'Yes, I do! At least, Jonathan won't turn up while we're here. When Nicola was talking to him in the Monmouth bar, he told her he had to work near London until this coming Friday. We should try and somehow mention the word "husband" to Heather and then see how she reacts. It's an innocent question. Remember, we are total strangers to her. She doesn't know how much we know about her and Jonathan!'

Helena and Susanna strolled along the wide main street, which was lined with detached houses of exactly the same design as *The Old Smithy*. This gave a pleasant uniform impression of solidity. All the houses were well-cared for, with an abundance of spring flowers in front, daffodils, tulips in flower beds, and wisteria twisting around and above front doors. Their cameras snapped many photos. Off the main street, they soon reached a footpath sign and decided to take it. It led along a field with sheep and lambs, led them through a small wood and up a hill from where they enjoyed a breathtaking view. They were really pleased with where they were, two lady detectives on a working holiday, or so they fancied!

They had a rest, then changed for dinner whose aroma drifted up the staircase and reminded them that they had somehow missed a bite for lunch earlier on. On entering the dining room and kitchen, they met a newly arrived couple in their thirties, Felix and Freya from Kent. After the introductions, Helena asked them how long they were staying in the B&B and learnt that they would be leaving on Thursday.

'So, will we be the only guests from Thursday to Friday, then?' Susanna asked Heather who confirms this.

'From Friday I won't be having any guests for a few days. I'm taking a breather,' she said.

Susanna and Helena exchanged glances, unnoticed by the others. Helena asked Freya and Felix what they did. Freya was a potter, and Felix was a chemist. They were asked in return what they did, and Susanna talked about her design company and Helena about her work on Belgian TV. Susanna now asked Heather what her husband did and commented that they had not met him yet.

'Oh, he works away from home quite a bit as a sound engineer, and he is away at the moment,' she said.

'How long have you been running your B&B?' Felix asked.

'A couple of years,' Heather replied, 'and I'm really enjoying it because of the company it gives me because my husband is away a lot.'

'It must keep you really busy if you have no helper, Heather,' said Helena, 'doing up the rooms when guests leave, doing the laundry and the ironing, not to forget the shopping for the breakfasts and evening meals, then the food preparation and clearing of the kitchen after.'

'Yes, it keeps me busy because I also look after the garden and have to exercise Dinah but then, I take a breather from time to time when I don't accept any bookings for a few days.'

'Can you recommend villages or towns to visit or some beauty spots in the countryside, Heather?'

Heather handed them all several brochures, and among other places recommended a visit to nearby Burford. The three-course dinner was very tasty, and the vegetables were from the garden.

Upstairs again in their room, Helena and Susanna studied the brochures more closely and made plans, a trip to Oxford on Tuesday, a walk in the countryside on Wednesday, and a visit to Burford on Thursday, hoping to find several antique shops where they could browse, and a cosy teashop for afternoon cream tea.

Heather even baked her own bread for breakfast and served up several jams she had made herself as well as marmalade. The eggs were from a nearby farm. The table was laid with a Villeroy and Boch *Naif* breakfast service with rustic scenes painted on. There were generous helpings of fresh fruit salad and yoghurt, different cereals, second and third cups of tea or coffee if wanted and the word, *generous,* seemed to go perfectly with Heather's character.

On Tuesday and Wednesday, they went on their outings and met up with Freya, Felix and Heather at the dinner table, and they shared impressions of the places they had visited during the day. These evenings were enjoyable, as well as nourishing. Heather was an excellent cook.

32

On Thursday morning, Helena and Susanna said goodbye to Freya and Felix after breakfast and took their time getting ready to leave for Burford which was just a few miles away. Heather stripped the bed in, *Seaweed*, where Felix and Freya had been staying, turned the washing machine on with their sheets and towels, cleaned the bathrooms and vacuum-cleaned the carpets in both, *Seaweed* and *Strawberry Thief* and tidied up the breakfast things in the kitchen.

She took Dinah out for a good hour. She felt lucky with her guests. Susanna and Helena were charming, friendly and appreciative, as Felix and Freya had been.

I must phone Sam in Burford for any news when I get back. I haven't done so for about ten days now, and I have to admit to myself that's because I'm petrified of bad news. I wouldn't have a clue what I'd do about that.

On her return home in the late morning, she first hung out the washing in the garden, then phoned Sam.

'Hello, it's Mrs Shilling here. I'm just wondering if you have any news.'

'Ah, Mrs Shilling, hello! If possible, I'd like you to come into the office today, perhaps in the early afternoon if you can manage?'

Heather's pulse had gone up at these words, and she was feeling sick to her stomach.

'Yes, you've obviously found something out. I'll be there, see you later, at about 2:30. Bye!'

As she was putting the phone down, she noticed how much she was trembling.

Helena and Susanna were enjoying a slow stroll down the streets of medieval Burford, with their cameras at the ready. There were so many beautiful motifs, so they stopped frequently. The main street sloped down to the willow-framed river Windrush and was lined with fine old houses and ancient cottages. The buildings leant picturesquely at precarious angles. From the top of the main street, you had beautiful views over the open countryside. There was an arched medieval bridge over the river. The shops had hardly changed since Tudor times. And there were wonderful little side streets to explore, with old pubs, tea shops and antique shops. There was a 15th-century parish church which looked magnificently impressive.

Susanna said, 'This is a sign of former riches based on wool, and I've also read that Burford was voted the sixth best place to live in Europe.'

They could picture themselves living here without any difficulties. The museum was housed in a Tudor building on stone pillars, and the wool merchants would have conducted their business transactions downstairs among the pillars. This was a wealthy town and still had a cared-for atmosphere.

They decided to indulge in a cream tea rather than having lunch but first they scoured the shops for unusual gifts to take back home. There were none of the boring, usual chains of shops, what a delight! In the first gift shop, Susanna bought

148

some handmade pottery, a mug in a beautiful rich blue. Helena found a hand-painted silk scarf in turquoise, blues and greens.

The next shop specialised in wood carvings, and both women bought a wooden pot stand consisting of three interlocking spirals which could be placed next to each other to accommodate a large hot casserole or pot. The stand was at its smallest when the spirals interlocked. Susanna was very taken by the design as she loved objects which could be arranged differently.

After a reinvigorating cup of coffee, they systematically combed the little antique shops which were stuffed full of mesmerising objects. They bought horse brasses, brass candlesticks from the eighteenth century, a couple of samplers, done by little girls as young as nine and eleven, and a silver teapot, milk jug and sugar bowl. Before they knew it, it was nearly 2 pm and they started the search for an inviting tea shop. They were extremely pleased with their purchases and could not stop smiling at each other and the people who were walking towards them. The tea shop they opted for had red and white checked curtains in the shop window. It must be popular as it was crowded with customers. They were lucky. When they entered, some people were just getting up to leave. On display on shelves along the walls, there were teapots of every possible design, period and décor which looked very attractive. They ordered their cream tea with Cornish clotted cream, and when it was served, they were confronted with the largest scones they had ever seen. The strawberry jam had large lumps of strawberries in it.

'Who was the strawberry thief?' Helena joked.

They wanted to stroll along the remaining side streets before they headed back to the B&B. Susanna suddenly nudged Helena with her elbow. On the opposite side, she had spotted Heather in front of a building with her back to them, studying the brass plates showing the names of the businesses inside. Heather disappeared into the building, and Susanna and Helena crossed the street and also looked at the brass plates. *Amy Miller, Chiropodist, ground floor*, *Peter Gardiner, Solicitor, first floor* and *Samuel Roberts, Private Investigator, second floor*, were written on them.

'I wonder which specialist Heather is seeing,' Helena said.

Susanna shrugged her shoulders. They were both intrigued beyond words. A number of new prospects were opening up.

'What if she is consulting a solicitor, Helena? Do you think she's seeking a divorce from Jonathan?'

'But how would she know about Nicola?'

'Let's get away from here before she comes out and sees us. Let's sit in the sunshine on a bench by the river.'

With the smoothly flowing river in front of them, they mused over this chance discovery.

'Let's hope, Heather is just having her feet seen to, Susanna.'

'I hope so, too, Helena, but what if she is seeing a solicitor? Is there any way that Heather could have got wind of Nicola?'

'Only, I think, if Matt has told Heather about Jonathan's affair with Nicola.'

150

'But a man would surely feel solidarity with another man, and above all, would never want to get involved in another man's business.'

'Yes, that sounds plausible, so it only leaves the private investigator.'

'How horrific just the thought of that is! A person must be pretty desperate to resort to a private investigator. I mean, there must be grounds for suspicion already, don't you think?'

'Yes, definitely! I can't wait to see Nicola's face tomorrow when we tell her!'

33

Heather could hardly drive herself home the few miles from Burford as her eyes were repeatedly filling with tears, which blurred her vision. Once at home, she got on Dinah and rode at a fast pace, almost hoping to fall off and break her neck. What she had learnt at Sam's office was more dreadful than she had anticipated. First of all, there was no girl or woman at the Acton office called Nicola as she had hoped. No, Nicola, the previous car owner, was Jonathan's lover and had been for quite a while, over a year, ever since he had bought Nicola's car for her. Tom, the subcontracted investigator in London, had done *good* work. That Thursday morning, Sam had received a large envelope at the office, containing a list of dates and places where Jonathan and Nicola had spent nights together recently, at her house whose address was well-known to Heather from the service record of her car, and at Matt's house in Denham. Worst of all had been the photos showing Jonathan leaving Nicola's house early in the morning, with his car parked in front of the house, and the two of them together at the pub in Denham, the ultimate proof. It was clearly visible that Jonathan was not wearing his wedding ring in this picture. What on earth was he playing at, pretending to Nicola that he was free? Heather had now had her first glimpse of Nicola, quite an attractive woman, dark-haired and slimmer than Heather, and possibly about the same age as Jonathan and Heather. The real nightmare was that Jonathan had broken his solemnly given pledge to be faithful, which she had been willing to accept as a completely serious undertaking on his part. He was repeating a pattern and that meant to Heather that it would be repeated evermore. She had to come to terms with the fact that he was a hopeless case, a cheat and philanderer. There were far-reaching implications, and she needed time to think about them before she made a decision.

She had asked Sam to keep the evidence in his office. There was no way that she wanted Jonathan to discover it in the house. She paid the last outstanding sum and terminated their arrangement, not without thanking Sam, in her pain still polite and adhering to conventions.

Heather was still ashamed that she had burst into tears in front of Sam who luckily had a box of tissues ready on his desk. Now she was, at last, free to cry and sob. Dinah turned her head as if to commiserate, which made Heather's tears flow even more. If only all the guests had gone! She dreaded Jonathan's arrival tomorrow. It would be hard to act naturally.

On her return from her ride, she saw her guests' car parked in front of the house. The two women seemed to be resting in their room after their excursion to Burford. Heather did not want to have dinner with them tonight. She would invent an excuse not to, perhaps pretending she had a stomach-ache or eaten something at lunchtime which had not agreed with her. If they had been her friends, she would have opened up to them, but they were strangers. She would phone her own friend Stella tonight.

When Susanna and Helena came down for dinner, they noticed Heather's red and swollen eyes and were feeling very sorry for her. Her not eating with them also confirmed to them that she had had shattering news. Her excuse sounded feeble. Heather was too straightforward to be a good actress. They fixed the time for breakfast before going up to their room where their discussion continued.

'Her swollen eyes must mean that she's either seen her solicitor or the private investigator and is downcast.'

'If I needed to place a bet, mine would be on the private investigator.'

'But we'll never know, so all our speculations are for nothing.'

They packed as much as possible to get away quickly after their 8:30 am breakfast the next morning.

Heather phoned Stella that evening.

'Hello?'

'It's Heather here, Stella.'

'Oh, Heather, to judge by your voice, you've had bad news, I can tell.'

'Yes, I have, Stella, worse than I could have imagined. There were reports by the man in London about when Jonathan and Nicola, that is the woman he bought my car from, met and where they spent nights together. What's more' – here Heather sobbed uncontrollably – 'is that there were photos as evidence, one of Jonathan leaving her house early in the morning, and one of them together at the pub in Denham, and their affair has been going on for over a year now.'

'I'm so, so sorry, Heather, to hear this. Would you like me to come over tonight?'

'No, thank you, Stella. Jonathan is due tomorrow for a few days, and I need to decide how to act in front of him, and what to say or not to say at this stage. I just feel I need so much more time to digest the news. It's really kind of you to offer, and I might well come back to it. Please, don't tell anyone about this, least of all Carol.'

'I'll keep this to myself, of course, Heather. Do take a sleeping tablet tonight, that's what I'd recommend.'

'Yes, that's a good idea. Bye, Stella!'

'Bye, Heather.'

34

In the morning, Susanna jumped out of bed and said a cheerful 'good morning' to Helena who was stretching and yawning. Susanna turned to the window and opened the linen Strawberry Thief curtains, then turned to Helena, gasping.

'Come here quickly, I don't trust my eyes, come and look at this! Oh, no!'

Helena took her time to climb out of bed, stretched again and yawned but was wide awake when she looked. Outside in front of the house was the well-known orange Mercedes!

'Heather was talking about taking a breather from today, and she said she does not take bookings from time to time. Perhaps this is connected with Jonathan's appearance, I'm just wondering why he is here already, I mean before we have left. He must have arrived in the middle of the night. Do you think he slept in the same bed as Heather?'

'I should think so and hope he's going to have a long lie-in this morning or will be doing something or other in one of the outhouses or sheds, so we won't see him, or he won't see us!'

'It'd serve him right if he sees us and in front of Heather who has no clue why we know each other!'

'I haven't got any idea how we should act. Do you think we can manage a cool "good morning" to him and can pretend we're meeting him the first time?'

'We'd be protecting him in that case. Even if we do, everything depends on his reaction to seeing us so unexpectedly. He might be the one to give the game away!'

It was after eleven o'clock on Thursday night. Heather had fallen asleep with the help of a sleeping tablet, exhausted from all her crying. Her bedroom door opened quietly, and she stirred when the eiderdown on the double bed was lifted. Though she was half-asleep, she registered with a shock that Jonathan had come home. He thought back to waking up next to Nicola in Denham this morning. And now he was in the same bed as Heather. How many men would envy him? Heather had not expected him until the next day. Her heart was hammering in her chest.

Jonathan whispered, 'I'm home, Heather. I was on my way to Denham on the A40 and then suddenly thought I might as well go from there onto the M40 and drive home. Are there any guests in the house?'

'Just two women who will be leaving after breakfast.'

'Ah, good! I'm so tired, see you in the morning!'

When Heather got up, Jonathan was still fast asleep. She was preparing breakfast for Susanna and Helena in the kitchen. They came down, as arranged, at 8:30 and first settled their bill with Heather, whose eyes still looked puffy. Helena and Susanna had nearly finished their breakfast when they heard floorboards creaking in the room above them. That could only be Jonathan. They exchanged looks and hoped he would be staying upstairs. But no, the kitchen door opened from the hallway, and Jonathan stepped in. He froze and seemed to go totally stiff and numb, with his eyes nearly popping out of their sockets. He swallowed.

It took him long moments to collect himself and keep himself from asking, 'What are you doing here?'

'Oh, hello, good morning,' he muttered.

Heather joined them by the table and introduced him as her husband. Susanna and Helena blushed as they were introduced to him but kept their cool.

Susanna and Helena got up and thanked Heather for a wonderful stay, wished her all the best and promised to recommend her B&B. They even gave her a hug.

Jonathan wanted to carry Helena's and Susanna's luggage down to their car.

Once outside the house, he did ask, 'What on earth are you doing here?'

Helena answered with a laugh. 'It's a free country, isn't it? Goodbye, Jonathan!'

Heather wanted to wave goodbye to them, stepped outside the house and heard them addressing her husband as *Jonathan*. She was puzzled that the one she introduced only as her *husband*, had given them his first name so quickly. In the car, Helena asked Susanna if she had also seen Jonathan wearing a wedding ring. She had missed that and was amazed to hear that. It seemed obvious that Jonathan sometimes pretended to be married, and sometimes that he was not.

These were five extremely difficult days for both Heather and Jonathan. Heather had been overwhelmed by a strong aversion to be touched by Jonathan. He sensed that something was quite wrong and wondered if Susanna and Helena had told Heather about Nicola and meeting him in Monmouth, and of course, he was too scared to ask. He was consumed by a massive bad conscience. He asked cautiously what the two Belgian ladies had been like, and Heather rather monosyllabically answered that they have been pleasant guests and that they had had interesting conversations over dinner every night. Jonathan's sensors were on, *alarm*. *Interesting* conversations? That could indeed mean that they had filled Heather in. Every night he tried to make it up to Heather by making love to her, the thing she wanted least. As she lay there, she wished she was the Queen bee and he a drone, because the drone's appendage would be ripped from his body during mating. Another strong image on her mind in those moments was that of a lamb led to slaughter.

He ignored her. 'Don't! Not tonight!'

The days were crawling by. Jonathan was aware that Heather was behaving differently. He asked what the matter is.

'Nothing,' replied Heather.

She knew she needed time to digest what she had found out and time to decide on how to proceed. Finally, Jonathan drove off. He had to work in France for a week.

'I'll phone you when I've arrived!' he shouted from the car.

35

Helena and Susanna had returned the hire car to the company in Chiswick and were sitting at the cosy kitchen table with Nicola, nursing cups of coffee. It was Friday afternoon, and the boys were still out. Later they would be off to a party. Just as well, as the three had a lot to talk about.

The most important point for Susanna and Helena was to impress on Nicola what a thoroughly decent woman Heather was:

'Listen, Nicola, there's absolutely nothing to hate or even dislike about her. She has been nothing but friendly and generous. She works very hard, without a helper, in the house and garden, and we reckon her life would be very lonely if it wasn't for her B&B guests. Here, we took a photo of her!'

Nicola snapped the photo out of Susanna's hand and took a deep breath, then admitted honestly:

'Yes, she really looks kind and likeable.'

The photo showed Heather and her horse, and Helena and Susanna also showed Nicola photos of their room, the house, the village and Burford.

Her friends pointed out again and again, 'Heather isn't your enemy, Nicola! On the contrary, Jonathan is the one who's stringing two women along. You probably won't believe it, but we've seen a wedding ring on Heather's and Jonathan's hands.'

Nicola gasped, 'What? Is that really true?'

Her friends nodded.

He had never worn a ring in her presence! He must still be married to Heather, then, in which case he was indeed treating both women abominably.

Nicola said, 'I've got a confession to make. I spent two nights with Jonathan since you'd left for the Cotswolds, one at my house, and one at Matt's.'

'That was a really bad relapse, Nicola,' they scolded her.

'I gave him that ultimatum which has just about another fortnight to run, and I wanted to remind him what he has in me!' she cried.

'You're a right fool, wanting the ultimatum to be decided in your favour, Nicola. You should pity Heather and give him up! Do tell us, were you followed when you went to Denham or did Jonathan say he was followed when he came to your house for the night? Have you ever had the feeling that you were being followed?'

Nicola was astonished. 'No, why?'

Her friends told her about spotting Heather in Burford where she either saw a solicitor or a private investigator and described Heather's red and swollen eyes later that day.

'Could she know your name, Nicola, and even your address?'

'Oh dear, yes, she could, from the service record of my car.'

'Be prepared to receive divorce papers citing you as co-respondent, Nicola, in the near future! Then you'll have to appear in court.'

Nicola was shocked. This was something she had not thought about at all. She knew she would have to think carefully about what outcome she wished for from the ultimatum.

Her friends were harsh in their admonishments, but she knew that they wanted to protect her from Jonathan. She was grateful to have such good friends.

After dinner, they adjourned to the living room and talked late into the night by candlelight and wine. They twisted and turned all the aspects of the *situation,* to and fro until there seemed nothing more to say.

To change the subject, Nicola mentioned the Hindu wedding she had been invited to again to her friends.

'The bride is one of my students who's recently joined my class. She's a very pretty sixteen-year-old with the longest hair I've ever seen. I'm very much looking forward to this wedding, which will be like no other I've ever been to. I've also been in touch with the local Red Cross office, and an instructor's available to come and teach First Aid to my class. I'm so excited because most of my students will have the chance of gaining the first certificate ever in their lives.'

The next day, Nicola drove her friends to Heathrow. She was not sure what to say to Jonathan when he rang her as promised from Milton-under-Wychwood. This time he had given as his reason for going there that Heather needed some wooden logs chopped for the fireplace. That was such a feeble explanation. Nicola was sure Jonathan was an accomplished liar.

36

Nicola had been given a week off teaching by Richard and enjoyed her mornings at the factory canteen. Her class had been split into two halves and had joined her two colleagues' classes during her absence. There were men and women working in this kitchen. She tried, without being in the way, to listen to any verbal exchanges among the kitchen staff and to the chef's instructions and explanations regarding the menu of the day while taking a lot of notes. She copied Health and Safety notices displayed on the walls. She noticed a First Aid box, and the chef explained that anybody cutting a finger had to put a blue plaster on this in case it dropped into the food, so it would then be highly visible, and the food would have to be discarded if that happened.

The lowliest job was that of the person who washed the pots and pans but would still be paid the hourly minimum wage for London. The staff went about their work quite cheerfully. She helped with dishing out lunches and snacks to the factory workers at lunchtime to collect more material for her linguistic analysis. At home in the afternoons, she was busy designing teaching materials.

She collected job advertisements for kitchen staff from newspapers to bring to class the following week.

When teaching the necessary vocabulary and structures on her return, it was predictably mostly the women in the class who seemed interested in working in a kitchen, based on their own experience of preparing food though Nicola stressed that men were also working in the kitchen she visited. Despite that, the men in her class adhered to traditional role divisions and did not seem interested but did the exercises like everybody else.

Those women with school-aged children did not want to work too far away from home.

Unfortunately, none of the kitchen vacancies in the newspapers were local. Nicola, therefore, offered to accompany those of her students who were interested in applying for such a job to the local job centre one afternoon and there was a good response. Not only that, but two of the women managed to get interviews and job offers in the canteen kitchen of a local factory. Nicola was very pleased, but to be realistic, this meant that only ten percent of her students were in work now.

She fared better with the idea of the First Aid certificate. Nicola had been in touch with a First Aid instructor who offered to come into her classroom on Monday, Wednesday and Friday for one week close to the end of the summer term. The first session was dedicated to the basic principles of First Aid which were to preserve life, to prevent deterioration, to promote recovery, calm down the situation, call for medical assistance and apply the relevant treatment. The instructor explained and demonstrated more about each principal and had brought charts along which stayed on the walls of the classroom for that week. The students were all ears and asked questions. Nicola was very pleased with the interest this had produced. Even if a student did not apply for a factory job, this was very important knowledge to save a life. The next session was for practice on how to dress wounds and bandage injured joints. The students worked in pairs to apply bandages and arm slings. As expected, women paired up with women and men with men. Next, the recovery position was practised. The instructor had brought a thin mattress, and Nicola volunteered to lie down on it and to have her body arranged into the recovery position by him. The students practised in the pairs they had formed previously. The instructor ended this second session by getting the students to repeat what had been taught so far. Participation was lively, and the students did well.

The Friday session was for the First Aid theoretical test, which all the students passed and was followed by a resuscitation exercise. The instructor had brought along a life-size rubber doll, which created a stir among the students. This doll was placed on the thin mattress, and the instructor knelt down beside it and demonstrated how to clear the airways, how to compress the chest and how to breathe into the mouth of this doll. He then cleaned the mouth of the doll with alcohol. The students seemed reluctant to fulfil this last part of the test before they could gain their certificate. Nicola, therefore, volunteered to do CPR on this doll, which did the trick: the students lined up to do the same. They were then immensely pleased to hold their certificate in their hands and waved it about in excitement. At the very end of the queue were three Muslim women who had watched their classmates in amazement and possibly in disbelief. They told Nicola that they could not do the resuscitation for religious reasons, something Nicola had not thought about. The women would not put their mouths where other people's mouths had been. The instructor came over and tried to assure these women that the mouth of the doll was sterilised with alcohol each time. The word *alcohol* was, of course, a red flag for any Muslim, and Nicola was very sorry that these three women would not be awarded a certificate. But the remaining fifteen students in her class were the proud owners of one.

37

George Hunter had stayed with Heather four or five times now, the first time for five days, and the others from a Friday night to Monday morning. His compilation of footpaths and bridle paths was going well, and he was enjoying this tremendously. She had always looked forward to seeing him again and had had the impression that he liked his stays with her. They had now been on first-name terms for quite a while. He was a caring sort of person. After each day's ride out on Dinah, he rubbed her down and brushed her, fed and watered her as though that went without saying. He had also examined her voluntarily and told Heather that her horse was in fine fettle. She was very moved that he took such an interest in the animal.

Jonathan had left for France. Her latest *breather* had been one long agony, with the nightly rapes. Yes, that's what she would like to call Jonathan's attacks on her in bed.

Jonathan would not listen when she told him, 'Don't, not tonight, please.'

Yet she could not bring herself to fight him in the knowledge that he was so much stronger than her, or he would have interrogated her. She was not ready to talk yet. She had not even had the time to reflect on all she had to absorb.

Today, George was due again for the weekend. Luckily, he was her only guest, a soothing thought. She felt at ease with him.

Over dinner on his first night, he remarked, 'Heather, you do seem a bit changed, and you appear to be quite preoccupied.'

She smiled shyly and admitted: 'Yes, I've got a lot to think about and actually will have to make a hard decision.'

George was very sensitive and did not persevere. He only asked, 'I've been wondering why I haven't seen your husband during any of my stays.'

She told him, 'He works away a lot and is in France for work now, and he doesn't like to have any guests in the house when he's home.'

George raised an eyebrow at that, and she shrugged.

After dinner, he went for a stroll through the village as usual while she tidied up the kitchen. It had become a habit for her to invite him for a nightcap in the living room on his return. And so, they were sitting in armchairs by the fireplace when she asked him about his family. At first, he seemed reluctant to talk but started after a lengthy pause.

'I was engaged to be married, but my fiancée died in an accident five years ago. The wedding was fixed for a date six months after her accident. We were so much looking forward to having a family. It took me a long time to learn to cope with her loss, and the fact is that I just haven't met the right woman to contemplate marriage again.'

Heather studied his face with deep interest, and she allowed her delight in his wish for children to blossom.

'What a sad thing to have happened,' Heather said in a soft voice, full of understanding and commiseration. 'I'm so sorry to hear that.'

She was looking at him, and he averted his face. She suspected that there were tears in his eyes. She started thinking about her predicament and suddenly could not stop herself from sobbing. George was alarmed and encouraged her to speak to him. Out tumbled words upon words, a torrent of words, accompanied by sobs, and she told him everything about her relationship with Jonathan, his previous affair, their separation and divorce, their reconciliation, his promises and her suspicions of his repeated cheating, his betrayal of her, her employing a private investigator and what she had found out only very recently, so recently that she had not had time to digest all the information, not to mention make a decision. She only knew that she could not ever trust her husband again, well, that he was not even her husband because they never remarried, so were still divorced.

George was a good listener, and when she had stopped talking for a while, he assured her, 'Heather, you can talk to me any time if it helps you to put words to feelings. What you've told me is safe with me and won't go further. You can phone me in Hinton where I live near Bristol whenever you feel the need.'

Now that they had exchanged intimate information about their lives, they felt closer to each other. Heather knew that she could trust George.

He asked her about children, thinking they might be away at Boarding School, and Heather dissolved in more tears and told George why there were no children, and that Jonathan had denied her any by adoption or artificial insemination as well. She ended by saying that it was probably too late now, with her almost in her mid-forties, but that she had come to terms with it. She added that she would go mad if she did not have the B&B because she liked looking after people and making them comfortable.

'I'm always looking forward to your next stay,' she said, and George added that his stays were a highlight he was looking forward to as well. They talked late into the night. When they said goodnight to each other on the landing, he gently stroked her cheek.

38

On the Sunday morning after their departure, the phone rang in Nicola's house. It was Susanna and Helena from Helena's house where the two families had gathered for lunch.

'It's us, Nicola, we got home okay. We're all at Helena's house for lunch. Many thanks for organising the trip and for having us in your house. It was the most thrilling holiday ever, we're contemplating changing our professions to becoming woman sleuths,' they said.

'Have there been any developments?'

Nicola told them that a furious Jonathan had phoned her on Saturday afternoon. 'He was absolutely livid, shouting at me and blaming me for having "planted" the two of you in his house, and the word "his" must have been a slip of the tongue! It seems that he owns it or owns it together with Heather, which would explain the wedding ring you spotted. I had no qualms at all to lie to him for a change, and so I claimed that you phoned the English Tourist Board from Belgium, asked for a B&B recommendation in the Cotswolds, and "The Old Smithy" was put forward, and then you made your booking by phone. I said it was pure coincidence and had nothing whatsoever to do with me. I also asked him if he was divorced or married, and there was just this long silence in reply. I think

I touched a nerve there. He just ignored my question, so I repeated that he'd told me he was divorced and that you two had seen a wedding ring on his finger in Milton. He mumbled, "Both." What is that supposed to mean? I also asked him if Heather really always had a breakdown, or if the ridiculous reason for his latest stay with her was to chop wood for her as he had told me. To finish, I reminded him that he had just ten days left to the ultimatum, and he said he'd be off to France in three days' time, and for a week, and he'd let me know on his return. He had calmed down a little by then and said, "Oh, Nicola", with a sigh.

'What an adventure, what a drama, Nicola! You'll keep us posted, won't you? Phone us anytime! Good luck.'

'Despite everything, I'm still in two minds about the answer to the ultimatum, I must confess, I mean what to wish for,' said Nicola. 'I've invested so much time and so many feelings in Jonathan!'

'He's a rat, Nicola, he doesn't deserve you, or Heather!'

39

Binita arrived from India fairly recently in Nicola's class. She had made friends with another young woman there, Daksha. Nicola saw them arriving and leaving together, and they sat next to each other in class. Binita was getting married at the end of the summer term and had invited Nicola. Nicola found out from her Hindu students that the date of the wedding was determined by astrology.

'Wear anything colourful for the wedding but not a red outfit. That for the bride! Red means love and passion. Weddings take three days, and the ceremony's done on day three with the reception after.'

When Nicola arrived at the temple, she was escorted to a seat in one of the front rows by Daksha. Nicola seemed to be the only non-Indian person there. What an honour! All the women there were wearing colourful saris in orange, yellow, green, turquoise, pink and blue. Nicola was wearing a long purple skirt and top, so was relieved that she fitted in.

The ceremony started with a procession of bridesmaids and groomsmen. They were paired up and walked down the aisle. Last to arrive by the altar were the male ring bearer and the flower girl. There was a canopy erected on a platform by the altar where a fire was burning.

When the bride arrived, Nicola saw that her hands showed the traditional intricate pattern which was applied by henna paste. She looked stunning in a brilliant red sari, worn with gold jewellery. Her husband, by her side, looked in his early thirties. He must have been twice his bride's age.

The wedding started with a prayer to Ganesh, the elephant God of good fortune. Then the newlyweds showered each other with rice, a symbol of fertility. The bride and groom also took seven steps together on the platform. They symbolised their commitment to each other, their future children, blessings for peace, health, friendship and loyalty, as well as respect and love for each other's families.

The bride was given three fistfuls of puffed rice which she threw into the fire. She had to shed some ceremonial tears which meant that she was sorry to leave her parents' house. The couple exchanged floral garlands but there was no kiss at the end of the ceremony because of the predominantly conservative culture.

At the reception, it was no surprise to Nicola that no alcohol was served.

At the beginning of the autumn term, Nicola was looking forward to seeing Binita and Daksha again. But Daksha arrived in class without her friend, so Nicola asked Daksha, 'Will Binita come in a bit later this morning, Daksha?'

Daksha seemed embarrassed and hesitant to talk more but Nicola asked her again about Binita.

Finally, Daksha said, 'Husband of Binita lock her in flat when go to work, she can't go out. He do shopping. Me no see Binita, last time wedding.'

Nicola was shocked at this disturbing news and would report this to Richard, the team leader. Before long, Binita was likely to be expecting her first baby. How could she bear this isolation?

40

The mutual outpourings between George and Heather had created a connection and a basis of trust between them. During breakfast on a Saturday morning, George wished that the two of them could go out riding together for the day, but regretted that Heather only had one horse, unfortunately.

'Oh,' said Heather, 'I can ring a neighbour, a farmer just a couple of miles away from here where I usually get my eggs. He has a good horse for riding and won't mind it being hired for the day. I'll give him a ring.'

George was delighted when Heather told him that it had all been arranged.

'I'll drive you there and will show you a shortcut away from the road for riding back here, and in the meantime, I'll have prepared a picnic lunch to take along.'

'How fantastic! Heather, don't bother with tidying my room this morning so we can get away as soon as I'm back.'

They spent a wonderful day together, riding quite a distance away from Milton-under-Wychwood in the sunshine. George made notes in his notebook and took photos from time to time, also asked Heather if he could take one of her on Dinah. There were streaks of sunlight on the foliage of trees, the spring flowers were out, and the path alternated along fields, through woods and along brooks. They stopped at one of them so the horses could drink, and they had lunch on a grassy knoll with a fine view. While eating, they shared a relaxing, companionable silence.

Then Heather explained about the financial situation, 'It's complicated. After our divorce, I bought Jonathan out by taking out a bank loan which I've been paying off from earnings from my B&B, and I had his name removed from the deeds, and after our reconciliation, he paid back the outstanding loan to the bank, and we had his name added to the deeds again. Ideally, I'd want to reverse these arrangements and be the sole owner of the house again, after what's happened. I want a clean break from Jonathan!'

George encouraged her to think along these lines. 'Yes, that's the best way to go about it, Heather.'

'But George, I dread the necessary confrontation with Jonathan and his unpredictable reaction, perhaps repeating pledges and promises which might weaken me again or becoming physically threatening.'

She was thinking of the recent nights with him she endured but could not mention it to George.

She laughed weakly. 'At least, I don't have to go through a divorce again because we're still divorced.'

George suggested, 'You should make an appointment to see the same bank manager as before as a first step.'

She had been banking her B&B takings with that very branch. Once she knew that she could borrow the money again to pay Jonathan the outstanding amount on his share of the house, she would surely feel more confident about the future.

George said, 'I'd recommend that you take your B&B accounts and tax returns with you to show from your average income that you can meet the monthly repayments. Once you've split from Jonathan for good, you can take guests again most of the time, so your earnings will be increased. You shouldn't have any financial worries.'

After the weekend, with George back in Hinton, Heather made an appointment to see the bank manager in Burford, taking her accounts and tax returns along. She explained that in future her earnings were likely to increase because she would be accepting guests most of the time. There was no problem with the loan, so she signed the relevant papers. It would take about ten days for the money to arrive in her account. During those ten days, she would have to finish her relationship with Jonathan, and face to face which she dreaded. She dropped by a hardware shop and bought two new locks, one for the front door, and one for the door leading from the kitchen into the garden. This was a purchase that fortified her resolve. She had spare padlocks for the outhouse and the garden shed at home.

Back there, she printed out a text on an A4 sheet of paper in readiness for Jonathan's next appearance.

41

During the week in Lille, Jonathan seemed somewhat disturbed to his colleagues. For the first time since they had known him, he did not fully concentrate and consequently made mistakes which affected the teamwork. Over a drink after work, they asked him if something was the matter, but he made light of it. Unusually, he left after just one drink, and his colleagues exchanged glances. He had a meal in a bistro by himself.

How on earth did I get into this situation with Heather and Nicola? Why can't I leave other women alone? Am I too daft to learn from the previous mess with Carol when I had to come begging to Heather? How strange that both 'lust' and 'love' are four-letter words! Do I love Nicola, do I love Heather or both of them? If so, do I love them equally? Which one do I love more, or do I love neither of them? I need to know because of Nicola's flipping ultimatum. Or is it mostly lust with Nicola? If I'm really honest with myself, the big attraction with Heather isn't love, it's the house and its surroundings and the feeling of leading a country gentleman's life. I know I'm hardly ever there but I'm thinking of my retirement. Also, Heather is so placid, she falls in with anything I do or suggest. It's just that she seemed a little out of sorts during my last stay. I hope to God, it had nothing to do with those two friends of Nicola's. I bet that Nicola booked her friends into the B&B on purpose though she denied it. Those so-called 'interesting' talks at the dinner table Heather mentioned, could Susanna and Helena have filled Heather in about Nicola and my appearance in Monmouth? But there was another couple staying, and it would have been another topic of interest, surely.

At the end of the week in France, Jonathan returned late at night and stayed at Matt's house. He rang Nicola the following evening.

'Hello?'

'Ah, Nicola, it's Jonathan here. How are you?'

'The ultimatum is up. Just tell me what you've decided.'

'Don't you even want to know how I got on in France?'

'No, I don't, so out with it!'

'This is a somewhat frosty welcome, Nicola! Well, if you want to know, I've decided that I can't decide.'

'And I have decided that I've finished with you, Jonathan Shilling! You've been stringing two women along, taking your wedding ring off when you're with me, and putting it back on when you're with Heather. You are obviously still married to her but pretended to me that you weren't. You're a fraud and a liar, you're despicable. I don't want you. I don't need you. I don't love you. Don't ring me again, don't knock on my door, this is it!'

She put the phone down. The relationship, which started with a phone call fittingly ended with a phone call.

Jonathan was stunned and could not believe what he had just heard. The shock made him sway, and he had to sit down. He did not even get a chance to assure Nicola that he and Heather were not married. She would not have believed the truth from someone who had told so many lies, anyway.

Nicola rang Helena straightaway. 'I'm so proud, Helena! I've just managed to finish with Jonathan!'

She repeated the words of her phone conversation with Jonathan.

'Helena, do tell Susanna the news as well. It hurts but I feel relieved.'

Helena commented, 'Jonathan's decision after the ultimatum is typically cowardly, in fact, it isn't a decision at all. He should be called "Mr Slimy".'

That evening, Nicola told Zac and Ben that she had made up her mind to drop Jonathan. They said that they had noticed that he did not make her happy and that this was therefore good news. They hugged her knowing that it could not have been easy for her.

42

Jonathan collected himself and calmed down, then rang Heather and announced that he would be coming home the following day. She asked what time she could expect him, and he said at 4 pm. Heather quickly phoned Stella and explained to her that she wanted to confront Jonathan and end her relationship with him but was aware there might be an unpredictable reaction. Stella agreed to Heather's request to come to *The Old Smithy* at 3 pm and sit in one of the guest rooms upstairs. If she heard screaming, she would enter the room downstairs where Heather was with Jonathan. Knowing about this safety net was very soothing for Heather.

The orange Mercedes drew up in front of *The Old Smithy*, shortly after 4 pm the next day. Jonathan took out his house keys, but they did not fit into the lock. He was puzzled, then realised that the lock had been changed. Furiously, he walked to the back of the house, confident that he could unlock the back door, but no! He returned to the front and rang the bell, and at the same time used the door knocker, making a lot of noise.

Heather answered the door and said, 'You're not welcome here anymore. This is the last time you will be entering this house. Come into the living room.'

Jonathan was perplexed and said, 'Whatever do you mean, Heather, this is my house as much as yours.'

'No longer, Jonathan, because you have betrayed me in the shabbiest way imaginable, and therefore I'm now "writing the script" and you will do as I say. I know that you have been in a relationship with the woman you bought my car from, and for more than a year. You cannot deny it because I have proof of you spending nights at her house and you sleeping with her at Matt's house.'

'What proof?'

'Just take it from me that I now know about what has been going on.'

Their voices were raised from time to time, and Stella got ready to dash downstairs if she heard screaming.

'Have Nicola's friends said anything to you when they stayed here recently?'

'Who do you mean?'

'You didn't realise then that Susanna and Helena from Belgium were Nicola's friends? Of course, they wouldn't have told you that! But I met them in Monmouth.'

'What on earth were you doing in Monmouth?'

'That's another story.'

'I know that you don't wear your wedding ring when you're away from here and only put it on when you are here. You pretended to Nicola that you were free. This is such a betrayal of the pledges and promises you made to me, and almost immediately after our second honeymoon, you started your affair with this Nicola. I despise you, you're weak and not trustworthy. You have now forfeited your last chance. It's over, Jonathan. How dare you misuse my trust like that? I now know that I will never trust you again, and it doesn't matter what vows and promises you invent, so don't even start begging me for another chance. This is what I've done: I've been to the bank and arranged for another loan, amounting to the sum, which was still outstanding when we made up. It's exactly the sum you paid back to the bank at that time. That sum will be in your bank account within a week or so. I've also drawn up an agreement you will sign to the effect that your name will be removed from the deeds of the house again.'

'There's no way I will do that, Heather!'

'Yes, you will, and it's right here. It is you who has destroyed our relationship, and I'm just so glad that we stayed divorced. If you refuse to sign, I'll go to the police and report you raping me the last time you stayed here, night after night.'

'I made love to you, Heather!'

'I asked you not to, and you forced yourself on me night after night.'

'There are always two sides to such a claim. But listen, Heather, I ended my relationship with Nicola.'

'Ah, so you admit having or having had a relationship with her! You ending it sounds such a coincidence that I can't believe that, knowing how many lies you've told in the past! It's more likely she finished her relationship with you! You can take all your clothes, your toolbox and other belongings with you from here after putting your signature on this piece of paper.'

And with that, Heather shoved the piece of paper in front of him and thinking about potentially having to appear in court on a rape charge, he signed on the dotted line that he agreed to his name being removed from the deeds. He had just signed away his beloved house and his dream of retiring to the countryside like a proper country squire.

He stormed upstairs to their bedroom, filled bags and a couple of suitcases with his belongings, took his toolbox from the outhouse, loaded his car and drove off, shouting to Heather, 'I didn't know what a bitch you are! Good riddance!'

In the car, out of sight, his tears rolled down his cheeks. His vision was blurred, and he had to stop by a field to collect himself.

Heather was agitated and felt drained. It was difficult for her to understand how smoothly this confrontation had gone in her favour. She had never been so determined and firm towards Jonathan. That was why he had not given her the respect she had wanted before.

Stella appeared from upstairs. She had been sitting in, *Strawberry Thief*, so had been able to overlook the street and see Jonathan drive off.

She hugged Heather. 'Can I make you a cup of tea, Heather?'

Heather related their final conversation to Stella while the two of them were sipping tea.

'I've always thought of him as unreliable, Heather, and I'm really happy on your behalf that you managed to cut the bond of such an unhealthy relationship. Perhaps one day you'll meet a much nicer, decent man, who knows?'

'Thank you for coming over, Stella, and your courageous readiness to intervene if necessary. Within a week or so, the house will be mine alone again. I can't believe it!'

43

The next day, Heather phoned George in Hinton. He was pleased to hear what Heather had achieved and suggested that she deserved a break after the high waves of emotion.

'You're more than welcome to come to Hinton for a few days, Heather. I think you need a change of scenery. Have you got guests booked in?'

'No, there was a chance I wouldn't succeed with Jonathan, and in that case, he'd have stayed here for a few days, so I hadn't taken any bookings.'

'Well, pack a bag and come to stay with me! I've seen you in your working life, and you can see me in mine.'

Heather arranged for Natalie next door to look after Dinah and was soon on her way. It was Friday, and George had told her that he and a colleague took it in turns to provide emergency service at the weekends, and he would be in charge of this coming one. She found his address easily. Hinton was a smaller village than Milton-under-Wychwood. He greeted her with a quick hug and a peck on her cheek. He had a cosy cottage, and she was relieved to see that he expected her to stay in a different bedroom to him, the cottage had just two. There was no pressure, she gratefully registered that. On arrival, he invited her into his kitchen with its low ceiling and made tea. Heather told him the details of the confrontation the day before. He was amazed at the drama in some people's lives. His had been relatively quiet in comparison, apart, of course, from the tragedy of his fiancée's death.

Heather had finished talking to an attentively listening George. She started looking around. On the kitchen dresser was a framed photo of Heather on Dinah. The discovery made Heather's heart jump.

'Come and stay with me next weekend, George, not as a guest but as my friend.'

'How about dinner at "the Bull" tonight?' George asked. Heather nodded and smiled.

Ingram Content Group UK Ltd.
Milton Keynes UK
UKHW020626160323
418667UK00014B/1242